Violet

A HISTORICAL NOVEL BASED ON THE LIFE OF

Violet Elizabeth Brown

By

Susan Elizabeth Buzard

With

Tracy K. Mayfield

Bloomington, IN   Milton Keynes, UK
authorHOUSE

AuthorHouse™
1663 Liberty Drive, Suite 200
Bloomington, IN 47403
www.authorhouse.com
Phone: 1-800-839-8640

AuthorHouse™ *UK Ltd.*
500 Avebury Boulevard
Central Milton Keynes, MK9 2BE
www.authorhouse.co.uk
Phone: 08001974150

© 2006 Susan Elizabeth Buzard. All rights reserved.

No part of this book may be reproduced, stored in a retrieval system, or transmitted by any means without the written permission of the author.

First published by AuthorHouse 3/10/2006

ISBN: 1-4259-1423-3 (sc)

Library of Congress Control Number: 2006900478

Printed in the United States of America
Bloomington, Indiana

This book is printed on acid-free paper.

The Poetry of the Negro
1746-1949
Langston Hughes
Ana Bontemps

Copyright 1949
Garden City, New York
The Country Life Press

"Trifle" by Georgia Douglas Johnson

"Dream Song" by Lewis Alexander

All pictures courtesy of the Coffeyville Historical Society - Propery of the Brown Mansion.

A portion of the proceeds of each sale of this book will be donated to preserve the Brown Mansion.

Acknowledgements

The idea for "Violet" started as a mere conversation on a rainy Sunday afternoon. One of those "I can't believe no one has ever written about Violet Brown's life - there is such a story there" kind of a deal. When you come from a small town and grow up seeing this mansion on a hill with all the mystery that surrounds it you can't help but be intrigued with the people who lived there. By the time I was old enough to have memories of the Brown Mansion it was in sad disrepair and had the look of a haunted house. Violet was old, sick and very much alone except for her housekeeper and her pets. What an opportunity it would have been to have spoken with her years ago instead of only being able to listen to interviews of her on audiotape. She was quite a lady.

I couldn't have written this book without the help of so many people and I want to thank them personally at this time. For those of you I unintentionally leave out, please accept my apologies. I spoke with so many wonderful people in my community and outside of it who went out of their way to help with this endeavor.

First of all I want to thank Tracy Mayfield for teaching me how to research one hundred years into the past. If it weren't for Tracy I never would have had the confidence to try this.

Thank you: To all the women at the Coffeyville Public Library: Karyl Buffington, Linda Shafer, Linda McFall, Joy Duvall, Cindy Powell and Elaine Wylie. You will never know how much I learned while spending so many hours with you. The late Mary Maud Read who provided me with hours of enjoyment while she bathed my mind in stories of the past. There was no one she didn't know and gave me ideas for many story lines throughout the book. Buck Warner who worked for the Brown's as a young man and told me stories that brought W.P. and Nannie K. Brown to life for me as we sat in his living room one cold winter morning. All the people associated with the Brown Mansion today as tour guides and members of the Historical Society, especially Lou Barndollar who gave me unlimited access to the mansion and permission to go through personal items and spend hours on the property sitting on the veranda writing. Fred Tillery, docent and caretaker of the mansion, who took me inside this wonderful home countless times so I could visualize certain ideas in my mind while telling me stories he himself had learned of. The people I had to contact from out of town who were so willing to help: Beccy Tanner and Sherry Chisenhall from the Wichita Eagle newspaper; Mike Kelly and Mary Nelson from Wichita State University. Holly Labossiere of the Ponca City Library. Valdine C. Atwood, a local historian in Machias, Maine, who I was able to learn about Violet's summer home in Machiasport, Maine, which is reported to be one of the oldest homes in the area, built in 1776. It is still there by the way and is a B&B owned and operated by the family who bought the home from Violet.

Most of all I want to acknowledge my family who were a constant source of encouragement and support during the writing of "Violet." You can't embark on an endeavor of this magnitude without their love and commitment in helping me see this through. They are: My mother, Louise Williams Swiger; my sisters, Sandy and Debbie; and most of all my children, Angela Elizabeth, Christopher Steven and Shane Jacob.

DISCLAIMER

    This novel can be described as historical fiction that is a tribute to a bygone era. For the most part, I stayed with the factual lives of Violet and the Brown family, but at times my imagination would race ahead to what might have been, perhaps was, secrets no one will ever know.

DEDICATION

    Violet, this story is told for you. Although I never knew you in life, your letters and documents introduced me to your triumphs and your tragedies. As I held these in my hands and walked the grounds of the mansion, I felt you beside me urging me to tell your story. Thank you for the legacy of the Brown Mansion and your enduring gift of treasured memories from one woman to another, one century to another.

Introduction

In the late 1800s, architect Stanford White designed and built a grand home in Coffeyville, Kansas, for W.P. Brown, a prominent oil and gas magnate. W.P. lived in the home with his wife, Nannie K., daughter, Violet and her younger brother, Donald. Today, that home stands atop a hill, alone and isolated except for the memories of Violet...

It is near the end of her life and Violet is on the brink of losing the mansion where she has lived for more than seventy years. Her father's dream had been to open it to the public after his death. She is in poor health and fearful of what will become of her. But, even more, she fears what will become of her home, known for miles around as the Brown Mansion.   Violet's story . . .

Trifle

Against the day of sorrow

Lay by some trifling thing

A smile, a kiss, a flower

For sweet remembering.

Then when the day is darkest

Without one rift of blue

Take out your little trifle

And dream your dream anew

by Georgia Douglas Johnson

in *The Poetry of the Negro (1746-1949)*

Chapter I

The boy took a sharp right and cruised to a stop in front of the pop machine. By the time he finished his paper route, the only thing in the whole world he wanted was a grape NEHI. It was pretty much routine for him to pull into the gas station for a cold pop on warm afternoons in the small town of Coffeyville, Kansas.

Standing with his back against the wall, Joe Williams wiped his greasy hands back and forth on an already too-greasy shop rag while awaiting his daily visit with Darby. He enjoyed watching the young boy come riding up to the station on his Sting Ray bike with the banana seat, sissy bar, and butterfly handlebars, all smiles and good-natured. Darby's visit allowed him, just for a minute, to feel young and innocent again with his whole life ahead of him.

"What's up, Joe?" Darby asked as he leaned off his bike, pushed at the kickstand with the toe of his sneaker, and reached into his pocket for change.

"Summer's about over, that's what's up," Joe answered. "Always makes me a little sad to see it go."

"Not me," said Darby. "I'm ready for fall. Football practice is my favorite class."

"Won't be long and all the trees will be turning up there at the mansion," Joe said glancing across the road.

"That place gives me the serious creeps," Darby whispered. "Some of my friends say it's haunted!"

"If it is haunted, it's only by memories. That old house has seen more than its share of sorrow."

Across the road stood the massive old house that everyone in town had always referred to as "the mansion." It belonged to the Brown family, and at one time had stood tall and proud on five hundred acres of prime farmland. Now, it looked forlorn, as if no one had loved or cared for it in years.

Vines strangled the huge columns on the once-inviting terrace, and the stucco exterior, suffering from the ravages of time, now cracked with areas where the paint had faded and chipped away.

The once beautiful gardens had been menacingly taken over with weeds strangling any hopeful bud. Volunteer trees had sprung up everywhere and the honeysuckle vines, planted nearly a hundred years before with love and care, now crawled undisciplined along the tops of the wrought iron fences.

The large house looked as though it had cried its last tears, years before, and had now given up all hope of ever being the grand "mansion" it had once been. Finishing his NEHI, Darby casually pushed the bottle into the waiting wooden crate used for the return of empty pop bottles.

"Well, Joe," he declared, "I better just get myself across the road and deliver my last paper to the mansion and get on home." Darby always left the big house on the hill for last. It made his heart pound and legs feel all shaky to have to pull up to the gates. There were always snarling Airedales that patrolled the property of the mansion.

"You be careful, Darb," Joe replied. "See you tomorrow?"

"Sure thing Joe," Darby smiled. As he approached the mansion, he thought again that it looked like the White House, but smaller and very sad.

With his last paper thrown, the sound of the vicious barking and snarling of the dogs faded away behind him. Darby pedaled as fast as he could back into town, while the silent mansion gathered itself into the shadows of the approaching night.

Pulling the shawl tighter around her shoulders as the late Indian summer afternoon began to chill, Violet knew the days were getting shorter and shorter, and the warmth from the sunshine just wasn't enough to warm her fragile bones anymore. *Where has my life gone?* she thought. *How could it have passed me by so quickly?*

Rocking slowly, back and forth in the old wicker rocker she watched the sun sink into the west. From the spacious veranda that surrounded the mansion, Violet could see all the land that had belonged to her family, all the way to the Verdigris River.

"Don't you think it's time to go in, Miss Violet?" Lemon asked, coming out to check on her.

"I could light us a fire in the library, and fix us some tea. How does that sound?"

Violet was too far away in her thoughts to even hear, so Lemon went in and started the tea.

"If only I could put my mind to rest today," Violet murmured to herself. "Why do all these thoughts of the past keep haunting me? Will there never be any peace in this old house?"

She rocked just a little more, not wanting to leave the beautiful sunset, but knowing the darkness was quickly approaching, and her tired old bones couldn't take the chill. *This was always the prettiest time of day at the mansion*, she thought. On summer evenings, Donald had chased fireflies across the carefully manicured lawn, while she smiled her older sister, indulgent smile. Now there were so many weeds that she couldn't get anyone to even mow it.

Reluctantly rising from the rocker, she looked out over the land once more. She could see what remained of her mother's greenhouse in the gathering shadows to the east. Oh, how proud she had always been of it.

I'm the only one left, Violet thought. *I've been the only one left for such a long time now.* Slowly, she walked over to the beveled glass French doors that led to the music room of the mansion. As she entered the doors and gazed at the beautiful grand piano it was as though she could hear the melodies of so long ago. Memories began to flood her consciousness once more…memories of the past bombarded her brain, complete with the sights, sounds and smells of years gone by.

"We were the Browns," Violet announced aloud in her tired papery-thin voice. She repeated again to the empty room, "We were the Browns!"

Thoughts assailed her as she slowly walked to the library. They had nagged her all day. *What would Papa have done?* It was maddening to think that if she had done just one small thing differently, she would not be in the position in which she now found herself. If…

If her father hadn't died at such a critical moment in history. If she had married a more capable man. If her education had been in business or law. If Mildred hadn't died. If...

Violet was tired of those "ifs," but they kept rolling around in her mind. When would she be able to let go of them and think of other things? She needed the "ifs" to leave her alone for a while so that she could make some plans.

How am I going to keep the house? Where will I get the money to fix the leak in the roof above the stairwell? If only I had kept a better eye on those workmen, they wouldn't have damaged the sealant on the terrace! Violet was obsessing, again, and feeling guilty about that as she did so many things. Maybe, if she tried hard enough, she could remember a time when the terrace had given her pleasure.

Roland's face came back to her and she remembered their first dance together, not what had come later. He had beautiful hazel eyes and dark blond hair. Though he had a fair complexion he had never burned in the summer, just turned a tawny color, and, Lord, have Mercy, how she had loved his skin!

On that golden summer night, they had danced almost every waltz and her ivory colored dress had flowed around the floor. It was effortless dancing with him, and when he led her out onto the terrace, she had gone willingly.

Paper lanterns had hung along the roofline, over the doorway. Momma had planned the party, and the house was all dressed up in its finest summer decorations.

Outside the night had been blessedly cool, with a breeze from the north. As they had approached the rail, he drew her into his arms, to keep her warm, he had said. It was what she had hoped for, and dreaded a little, too.

She was always a little self-conscious of her height and she certainly didn't have her mother's tiny waist. It had been her cross to bear for much of her life, ever since she started growing taller and taller around her eleventh year. It seemed everyone was always remarking about how her legs weren't "shaped" like her momma's, and, of course, it didn't take her long to realize they were referring to the fact that her calves didn't curve in to delicate little ankles and small feet. Not to mention the fact that her momma, Nannie K. Brown, had a seventeen-inch waistline!

Simply put, Violet had grown to be tall and rather large-boned compared to her momma's petite frame of 4'11." She had accepted it at some point, but it still stung once in awhile, and she always felt self-conscious no matter how she tried to reassure herself it was all right to have taken after her father.

"Oh, here you are," said Lemon, "I was just coming out to get you. I have our tea all ready and the fire's going too. Is there something wrong, Miss Violet? Are you feeling all right?"

Violet, feeling mildly annoyed at having been interrupted in her memories, replied, "I'm fine, Lemon. I'm just worried, that's all. I've got some decisions that need to be made and the sooner the better." They both sat down next to the fire, and while Lemon poured the tea, Violet began to speak, haltingly at first, but then gaining speed, as her thoughts came together.

"Lemon," Violet said slowly, "I can't remember a time when you weren't with my family. As far back as my memory will reach, you've always been here. I don't recall if I've ever asked you if you were happy here or if there wasn't something else you'd rather have been doing."

"Oh, I've always been happy working for your family, Miss Violet," Lemon replied. "I've had a right fine life, as a matter of fact."

"The reason I'm bringing this up now, Lemon, is that I trust you, and it's important that you know that. I know I haven't always been the easiest person to work for, and for that I hope you'll understand I've tried to make the best of some pretty bad situations."

"I sure know that, Miss Violet. Now you just quit your worrying and let's have our tea."

"No...no, Lemon, you need to understand."

"Understand what, Miss Violet?"

"We're running out of time, Lemon. We've almost completely run out of time.

It's been thirty-five years since Momma and Papa died. It's almost 1970, Lemon. Almost forty-one years since the crash when Papa darn near lost everything, we had. I've been selling off the land little by little, you know I have, and I just can't bear the thought of having to sell any more.

"Papa would turn over in his grave if he knew I was so desperate a couple of years ago I sold that land down the hill to that man who built a trailer park. Good Lord, Lemon, a trailer park, of all things. It makes me tremble all over to know that someday I have to see Papa again and answer for that one."

"He understands, Miss Violet."

"I doubt that, Lemon, but the point I'm trying to make is that unless I can think of a way to increase my income and do it quickly, there's no telling what I'll have to do next."

"Oh, for goodness sake, Miss Violet, we've been through tougher times than this. You've just forgotten is all, this isn't something we can't get through. Why, there was a time when I remember your momma and papa having some awful tough decisions to make. Course, you were either too little or living elsewhere, to even remember some of them. You were only a little bitty thing when I came to work for your parents. Lord, let me think. That's been a lifetime ago."

"Is there anything back there you can remember that's good, Lemon?

I really need something good right about now so I can make it through the rest of this day."

"Well, Miss Violet, I don't know how good it all was, my memory's not what it used to be, but I'm sure to remember a few things that'll cheer you up. Then there will be those that'll have us both crying, as well."

"Oh, Lemon, do we dare go back and revisit it all?"

"It'll be all right, don't you fret none. I'm here," Lemon said soothingly. "I'm here."

Lemon refreshed their cups with the hot Earl Grey tea Violet loved so well, and they settled comfortably into their favorite chairs and began the journey…down the path to their youth.

"Miss Violet, I wasn't always with your family. Sometimes I lived here at the mansion, but other times I came during the day, and went to my own home at night. There was even a few years that I didn't work at all, 'cause I was raising my children and caring for my husband, when he got sick.

"When the trolley tracks came down Walnut Street, I started sleeping at home. My mamma took care of my children when I was working, but they needed to have me around, too."

"How are your children?"

"They're getting old like us, Miss Violet," and she chuckled a little.

"I've got three great-grand children. Next spring I'm going to visit every one of my children. They bought me a plane ticket, so's I can stop for a week at each of their homes! Spend time with all my grandchildren and great-grandchildren.

"Did you ever hear such a thing? Me flying from city to city like a stewardess or someone on a "grand tour."! She shook her head in disbelief.

"You've earned it, Lemon. You raised and educated your children. I have never heard anyone say a single word of criticism of your children. Be proud of them," and she paused. "There have been many times when I envied you."

"Me? Miss Violet."

"You had a loving husband and three children. Of course, I envied you. At the same time, I was so glad for you."

"I'm sorry. I didn't think about what I was saying, bragging like that." Lemon put her hand on Violet's arm.

"Nonsense. You be happy and proud!" Violet paused for a moment, lost in thought.

Then she spoke of her life, family, and even a little about her marriages. And she listened to Lemon, learning a great deal more about her family than she had ever known, until the sound of a nearby hoot owl announced the lateness of the hour. Violet realized that she had revealed more than she had ever shared with another soul. And it felt good...it felt *right*.

"I'd better get out of this chair and into bed, before I get any stiffer." Violet's hands were on the arms of the winged back chair, pushing her self up.

Lemon rose to help Violet and she let her, but all the way to her room she made self-deprecating noises, insisting that she did not need help preparing for bed.

Being close to eighty-seven years of age, Violet couldn't believe that Lemon was seven years older than she was. Slighter of build, Lemon had always been active and seemed to enjoy good health, never showing any signs of slowing down.

In the morning, she'd have to figure out what to do. Lemon couldn't keep on taking care of her, and she didn't see how she'd be able to pay a full-time person to live with her.

As Lemon was helping her into the hospital bed, Violet was thinking. *How much longer will I be able to walk? What will I do if I'm confined to bed?*

"We'll talk some more come morning, all right, Lemon?" Violet implored.

"Sure we will, Miss Violet. Right now you just rest yourself. I'll see you in the morning."

Violet shoved all those nagging questions away and sighing deeply, slowly relaxed into the comfortable bed.

What would Papa think if he knew his billiard room is now my bedroom?

Again, with great effort, she pushed away all the worries that she could. Taking in a long, deep breath, Violet softly blew it out in one long exhale. Consciously relaxing her tight shoulder muscles, she began to settle down. It was quiet now and she knew Lemon had gone to the kitchen.

Probably she was washing up the tea things before retiring to the little room, just off the kitchen that had once been used as the staff dining room – the room where Mildred had died.

And very gently, Violet slid into the welcome dusk of sleep.

Chapter II

Violet opened her eyes and turned her head toward the window. For weeks now, it seemed she had been waking earlier and earlier.

"It's all this damn worrying," she mumbled to herself. "A body can't rest with a ton of problems to solve."

She gradually began making the transition from the bed to a standing position; a process that seemed more trouble than it was worth with arthritis and other accompanying aches and pains of old age becoming a reality with each passing day.

With deep sighs, Violet pulled on her robe and slipped her feet into her worn, but comfortable slippers. She walked to the dresser, and as she reached down to pick up her hairbrush, she saw her reflection looking back at her from the mirror. She thought for what seemed the hundredth time lately, W*ho is that old woman? How can this be?* Violet was deeply depressed and losing ground rapidly. She turned away from the mirror, disgusted and angry.

She opened her bedroom door and smelled the aroma of coffee and bacon. She couldn't help but smile. Only Lemon would think that food could solve all the world's problems.

Violet entered the grand dining room of the mansion without seeing it at all. She hadn't thought about the grandeur of the house for many years. The room was open and large with French doors opening to the veranda on the south. The rectangular windows above those doors bore hand-painted grapevines in beautiful shades of amethyst and green. There was a fireplace on the east wall of the dining room and the entire north wall contained a recessed china cabinet filled with the world's most beautiful china and glassware. The stained glass chandelier that hung over the dining room table was not only designed and autographed by Louis Tiffany; he personally came and hung the massive light in the home as well.

"I was just coming to get you, Miss Violet." Lemon exclaimed. She sat the platter down on the table and hurried over to help Violet.

"Even age hasn't dimmed that cheerfulness of yours, Lemon." Violet complained, scowling.

"Oh, now, you come on over here and have some of my bacon and eggs, and that will cheer you right up." Lemon grinned.

"I have every right to be grouchy, Lemon. I'm old, I'm broke, and even your bacon and eggs, as wonderful as they are, can't change that fact." Violet winced as every joint reminded her of its antiquity as she lowered herself onto the chair.

"We're going to figure everything out, Miss Violet. We always have. Now let's get some food in our stomachs, all right?" Lemon poured coffee into both their cups, and spooned a generous portion of scrambled eggs onto the china plate in front of Violet.

As Violet raised the cup of hot steaming coffee to her mouth, she paused and looked at the intricate china cup in her hand. She had a faraway look in her eye as she said; "This china was given to my parents on their wedding day, Lemon."

"It sure was, Miss Violet, and absolutely gorgeous too." Lemon offered.

"Have you ever heard the story of how my parents met?" Violet asked. "It was quite romantic. Momma loved telling me about their early years together."

"I've long since forgotten. This old mind has to work a lot harder nowadays." Lemon laughed.

"Lord, don't I know it." Violet agreed.

They both began to eat their breakfast and in between bites of scrambled eggs and sips of coffee, Violet told Lemon the story of her parents' first meeting all those years before.

William Pitzer Brown, known to his friends as W.P., had been at a small social gathering in Independence, Kansas, not more than twenty miles from Coffeyville, playing Whist, when someone started playing the piano behind him. He turned and looked to see who it was. All that was visible was the top of a young woman's head, covered in tiny curls of auburn hair. Just above the sheet music, he caught a glimpse of a creamy pink complexion. W.P. had to stand up to see what the rest of this petite young lady looked like. He caught a flash of dark eyes, and he was hooked.

When he reached the piano, he found a tiny woman, dressed in linen, with frothy lace down the front of her gown. The sleeves above her wrists were tight, and he thought her arms must be the size of a ten-year-old girl. Small hands were producing the melody with vigor and a volume that was surprising. Just as he turned to ask his friend, John Kloehr, about her, she looked at him again and he was lost in those deeply hazel eyes. Flashing him a smile, she returned to her music and seemed content with it, not needing his or anyone's company. In that momentary glance, he had seen good humor and determination. No one would ever get the best of this woman, he thought.

And his heart was gone.

He had been on his own for about six years, first working in a bank and now he made money brokering grain sales. W.P.'s father, the General, had been a harsh parent, not drilling his children, as he would have his soldiers. No, he just expected them to get it right immediately, and was quick to punish if they didn't.

By the time W.P. had turned sixteen, he was out of the house, having decided if he were to fail at anything, he'd be the one who decided his fate, not his father.

Now, he had money in the bank and was in the process of buying some land in Montgomery County, Kansas.

A hand on his sleeve announced the arrival of his friend John.

"It's not polite to stare, Mr. Brown." There was a tone of "I told you so" in his voice. Last year John had found a marvelous girl and W.P. had made fun of his behavior, at the time. John was glad to be able to tease his friend for a change.

"Keep your mind on business, John," the hardworking Mr. Brown, had told him when John had found his future wife, Hattie Eldridge. "You'll never get anywhere if you lose your head with some female creature."

Now John poked W.P. in the ribs and asked, "Where's your head, old man? It's time to go out back."

Somehow, W.P. managed to turn from the vision and went out through the dining room and kitchen to join the other young men standing in a circle, while they shared a nip or two from a small flask.

"Who is that girl at the piano?"

More than one voice intoned the answer.

"Nancy Kilgore from Ohio."

"Don't get attached, she's going home in a couple of days. You'll never see her again."

"Yes, I will." And he meant it.

After following her back to Port Washington, Ohio, he had courted her, won her hand, and brought her to Independence, Kansas. His bachelor abode, a room over the local baker, hadn't seemed appropriate for such a well brought up young woman from a well-to-to family, so he had swallowed his pride, and asked his parents if they could stay with them for "awhile."

Within eighteen months, he had moved his pretty wife, who he referred to as Nannie K., and their new daughter, into an apartment above the lumberyard, which he had purchased in Coffeyville, twenty miles to the southeast of Independence.

His grain brokerage was still bringing in a good income, the lumber business was booming, and he had a beautiful little family; and he was only twenty-four.

The Kilgore's were impressed, too, and invested in his businesses. Everything was going so well.

Secretly, he suspected that the Kilgore's had approved of him because his father was General William R. Brown, Retired, of the Union Army. Mr. Kilgore's principal business was a tannery that had supplied much of the leather used by the northern forces.

But marrying Nannie was so important to him that their disapproval would have been of no consequence to him. Nannie K. would have been very hesitant to override her parents' wishes, but his love for her would have won the day. Of that, he was certain.

Then, there was Violet. Born in early July 1885, and named after W.P.'s mother, Violetta, she was adorable and adored from the first day. When Nannie K. couldn't produce enough milk to nurse her adequately, W.P. hired the finest wet-nurse he could find.

Being W.P., he also bought three milk cows and hired a small boy to take them daily to the common grazing area, Osborne's Pasture, not far north of the downtown plaza. This occasioned much speculation from the townspeople who weren't used to one household having three pedigreed cows, two Jerseys, and a Guernsey.

The Browns were new to Coffeyville, though some were aware that W.P. owned a farm two miles south of town. Tall and always well dressed, W.P. was soon identified as the owner of the new cows, and when they were brought home to the stable behind the lumberyard each evening, more than one shook his head. If all you wanted was some good milk and cream, any crossbred cow would do, and no household could use as much milk as three cows could produce.

He was surely a businessman with plans, some said, and people began to take note of Mr. W.P. Brown.

As soon as her mother pronounced Violet old enough to go out, W.P. was seen walking around town with the small child in his arms. He showed her anything in which she was the least interested, and explained everything to her, as he would have to a much older child.

Soon, Nannie K. and W.P. were being invited to most of the social functions in town. Being a sworn Democrat, he understood when the Republicans didn't invite him to their political/social gatherings. Nor did he invite Republicans to his home.

Being of a gregarious nature and very intelligent, W.P. could talk to anyone about anything. Having strong opinions on everything, and not willing to compromise on most things, his ability to speak would not be used in politics, as his father's was. General William R. Brown was County Commissioner.

W.P. joined social clubs for men, including so-called "secret societies" whose officers, meetings, and gatherings were all announced in the local paper, *The Journal*. There was at least one "hunting club" and this group was truly secret, leading to the speculation that it was a local group of the KKK. The officers and members of the "hunting club" were not published. Another interesting group was the "anti-horse thief society," which wreaked vigilante justice on persons of color.

W.P.'s name was never associated with the "hunting club" or the "anti-horse thief society.""

Nannnie K. also joined some groups, for ladies, but being a new and dedicated mother she didn't like to spend much time away from Violet. After a second pregnancy ended at almost full term, they laid the baby boy in the family plot, which W.P. had purchased for them in Elmwood Cemetery and Nannie K. spent even more time with her daughter.

In the evenings, Nannie K. read to her little family and answered every question that Violet ever asked, fully and satisfyingly. Violet loved to sit in her father's lap and look into the flames in the fireplace in their sitting room. Her mother's words conjured pictures of adventurous heroes and women in ruby colored ball gowns in the flickering fire. Nobility, chivalrous deeds, wizards, and dragons all chased around in her head until she fell asleep in the safety of her father's arms. Sometimes, she would remember him tucking her into bed, but mostly she recalled waking up in the morning, feeling loved, protected, and like a princess coming out of a magical sleep.

For Violet, each day began with the Brown's housekeeper and cook, Maggie McElvry, washing her face and dressing her in simple, sturdy clothes. After breakfast, Maggie would carry a tray to Mrs. Brown, and then she would take Violet for a walk. "Taking the air" was good for children and grownups, but Nannie K. preferred taking her stroll in the afternoon.

One of her pleasures in life was sleeping until 8 or 9 o'clock, and having a breakfast tray on the small round table by the window. She liked to watch people passing by, intermingled with wagons and carriages. Occasionally, there was a herd of cattle, driven in from the Indian Territory, to the railhead in Coffeyville. Often she could identify many of the people from her window, like the Dalton boys bringing in a string of horses to sell. They were known for training horses and lived near W.P.'s farm just south of town. Bob Dalton had purchased a new wagon from Brown's Supply, W.P.'s lumberyard, and Violet, like any child, was always glad to see her friend, Mr. Bob Dalton, when he came into town. Nannie K. would sit and drink her coffee, taking note of the visitors to town, and reading the paper, which usually contained short works of fiction, as well as the news.

Sometimes she thought the entire paper looked like a work of fiction, with tales of lurid crimes from around the country, ads promising that various herbal potions could cure cancer, restore your hair and make you look fifteen years younger. The column that taught housewife skills and provided recipes was always interesting to read, though at times it advised doing things that sounded silly to her, such as, meeting your husband at the door with a cup of beef consume. The theory was that his day was more important and more tiring for the workingman, than it was for the wife who had stayed home and "worked."

There was plenty of crime to read about as well. Coffeyville was certainly no exception. There were murders, fights and thefts of all sorts. The frontier was far from tamed in the late 1800's.

The first actual settler at Coffeyville was a freed slave, Louis Scott. In 1869, he started farming near Onion Creek, and the Verdigris River. A few years later, Colonel Coffey arrived and started a trading post, mostly dealing with the Black Dog, Osage Tribe. He had over a dozen men with him; not the scouts of legend, or great hunters of buffalo. His group included doctors, lawyers, and merchants of every kind. Coffey's dealings with the Osage were friendly. He was honest and earned their respect.

The trading post with its clutter of other stores was restricting development of the town, so Coffey and those with him, went two miles north and laid out a plaza area. Here they built new stores, or moved the old ones into this more sensible arrangement.

This was a working town from the beginning. Supplies came down the Verdigris River by boat, or by wagon. In 1871, a railroad spur came to the west side of the river, to Coffeyville. This effectively killed the small town of Parker, which was on the east bank of the Verdigris. Parker began losing businesses, one after the other, as they were moved across the river to Coffeyville.

A remarkable doctor and a born leader of men, Dr. Thaddeus Frazier brought his four-year-old medical practice from Parker to Coffeyville in 1874. Dr. Frazier had served in the Confederate Army, in The War or the "Rebellion" as some called it. Wounded at Wilson Creek, his left arm had been amputated. Before the war, he had been training to be a doctor, and after the war he returned to his studies. He began his practice near Springfield, Missouri, not far from the Wilson Creek battlefield. When Colonel Coffey left to seek the new frontier to the West, Dr. Frazier became the Mayor and was re-elected several times. He was very active in city government and was an officer in many of the so-called "secret societies." He even built one of the first hospitals in Coffeyville.

Another physician who came to the new town of Coffeyville with Colonel Coffey was Dr. W.H. Wells. He loved to tell people the story of his unfortunate lack of timing as to find himself in a restaurant near the Ford Theatre at the time President Lincoln was shot.

Coffeyville suffered many evils, fires, floods, gas explosions, and of course, the Dalton Raid before the turn of the century. Yet, it was a growing town seemingly meant to become an important city in Kansas' history.

"Yes," said Violet, "This is the place where W.P. Brown, my Papa, brought his family, found his fortune, and built our home, this beautiful home. Why, even then, people talked about it for miles around."

Chapter III

"I'm going to clear this table and do up the dishes, Miss Violet. Why don't you go on into the library and rest awhile? You call if you need anything."

"That sounds like a good idea, Lemon. I'm going to put my feet up and read a bit. I've started a book, but just can't seem to get interested in it with all that's been on my mind. Maybe I'll try to read."

"There you go. That's a fine idea. I'll be back to check on you in a jiffy."

Violet watched Lemon walk slowly away, and noticed for the first time how slow her step had become. Her eyes followed Lemon until she could no longer see her, but she knew she had reached the kitchen. Violet imagined Lemon gazing up at the feeble light bulb over the kitchen sink so high above her head that it was virtually useless. She remembered installing that old light, just before Pearl Harbor, in 1941. She knew that Lemon would set about the task of washing up the breakfast dishes, humming while she worked. Her mind slipped back on its journey to the past once again…

Lemon had always enjoyed working for the Brown family. She had come to work for them when she was but twelve years old.

Her parents, Grant and Minnie Israel, had been one of the many "Exodusters" who fled the south after slavery was abolished, moving north to find their "Promised Land." They walked the whole way. A strong man of deep faith, Grant Israel knew God had set them free and would protect them on the journey. Many people fell by the wayside and crude markers were placed where they had been laid to rest. Coffeyville was still just a trading post when the Israel's arrived. Grant found a job loading and unloading wagons. Before long they had a little cabin built near Onion Creek. Lemon was born in that cabin. Grant and Minnie Israel were well thought of and respected members of the community.

One spring day, Grant Israel took his mule and rode off to help plow some land over by Clymore. It had taken Grant over a year to save up enough money for that mule. When he didn't return at the appointed time, Minnie knew something was wrong. A search party was dispatched and Grant's body was found the next day. They found his body about a hundred feet off the road, miles from home. He had been shot. The mule was nowhere to be found. His murder was never solved.

Minnie Israel was now a widow with three children. Lemon, being the oldest decided it was her responsibility to go to work. Minnie did laundry for the local ladies and that brought in a fair amount each week, but Lemon convinced her mother she could help even more, and went about finding work.

Isham Hardware was a store Lemon's father frequently visited for supplies, and Lemon had accompanied him on trips more than once, so that became the first stop on her list. Her first employment was for Mr. Isham's wife, who hadn't been well and needed cared for temporarily. Lemon did such a good job, she was highly recommended around town when Mrs. Isham was fully recuperated. She had learned to iron, do some light cooking, and to serve at dinner.

The Brown family had a five-year-old daughter and another baby on the way; and as Lemon had been so highly thought of by Mrs. Isham, W.P. Brown hired Lemon to help with Violet, and various chores around the house. Lemon and Violet were seven years apart in age, and Lemon thought Violet to be a most beautiful child with her blond curls and dark, sensitive eyes. Lemon had been with the Browns about a month when Mrs. Brown lost the tiny baby boy she had been carrying. Lemon had been very young, but she comprehended the loss to Mr. Brown and his beautiful wife, Nannie K. She concentrated all her efforts on caring for Violet as Violet's parents grieved the loss of their tiny son.

Violet knew that Lemon had spent the better part of her life worrying about Violet and, true, she had helped her out of more than one scrape and was glad to do it. Lemon loved Violet the way an older sister loves a younger one. Even though their skin was a different color, it mattered not in Violet's eyes. Violet knew that Lemon had seen to her for too many years to turn her back on her now. She would help her figure out what to do; there was no doubt in her mind.

Violet

Violet roamed the library, glancing over all the various titles in the stacks of books that lined the walls, many of which were leather bound first editions. She had tried to sit down and read, but the anxiety was too overwhelming, so she found herself to be up and about without really knowing what it was she was seeking. The library was placed centrally in the house, between the solarium and the music room. With a large bay window facing the south, the library was the perfect place to spend an afternoon with a good book. Reading was a favorite pastime among the Brown family. Wingback chairs were positioned on each side of an oval table (complete with secret drawer) upon which stood one of the most beautiful Tiffany lamps ever made. There sat the blue glazed Chinese lion dogs with their perpetual snarls that her mother had brought home from a trip to the Orient. The fireplace was lit and the gas-fed coals glowed warmly. This had been her father's favorite of the many fireplaces in the house. The small tiles of varying shades of light and deep jade green and the dark oak mantel above so complimented one another. This room had been well planned out for its purpose.

Violet's gaze lingered on a faded book, oversized from the others, and down on a lower shelf. It was an old photo album. She had leafed through its pages many times over the years, but in the past twenty or so years, the photo album had been left untouched. It had become too painful for Violet to look within its covers. There was happiness in there, certainly, but oh, so much pain as well, so much loss.

Violet reached for the old album and hugged it close to her heart as she moved toward the chair to sit down. Before she had even opened the cover, the first tears were forming and beginning to spill down her cheeks. One after another they marched like obedient soldiers in a straight line down her creased and aged face, only to fall one after another onto the discolored old book that held the memories of her family's lives.

Lemon appeared in the doorway and seeing Violet, with the familiar old book in her hands, went to her and knelt down beside her.

"Are you sure you want to look at that today, Miss Violet? It's been known to make you awful blue."

"I have to, Lemon. It's most likely the last time I'll ever look at it, as a matter of fact. How many years could I possibly have left? Fact is, I'm all used up, Lemon, and this old house along with me. All my father's dreams…gone. Everything he worked so hard for. I've done nothing but let him down."

"Don't say that, Miss Violet. You've done the very best you could, and besides, it's not over till the fat lady sings, right? I've always loved that old sayin'," Lemon chuckled. "But I doubt the opera singers have…all right then, let's have a look at these old photographs and just see if maybe we don't find the answer to what we're lookin' for down deep in one of these dusty old pages."

Down through the tunnel of time they went, like characters in *Alice in Wonderland*…back through history…back to when. . .

Coffeyville, Kansas, was becoming known across the country as "Gate City" and "Gateway to the West."

For my seventh birthday I asked for my very own pony. Luther Perkins son, Maurice, had gotten his own pony, and I wanted one too. Papa didn't much care for Mr. Perkins, for political reasons and personal differences, so he spoke to a common acquaintance to find out the location and breeder of Maurice's pony.

I had already shown promise of becoming quite a little horsewoman and could drive the pony cart. With the right mount, I reasoned to Papa, I could keep up with him when he rode out of town to check on the farm, two miles south of Coffeyville where papa raised cattle and sheep. Of course, he had to convince Momma that horseback riding was suitable physical exercise for young ladies. He was confident that she would give in once she saw me atop a good-looking pony.

Momma planned a birthday party. All my playmates and friends in town would be invited. The day of my birthday finally arrived, as hot and humid as July in Kansas can possibly be. Momma had asked one of the part-time ladies that sometimes helped out around the house to come in and help. This would mean that fourteen-year-old Lemon wouldn't have to take a turn on the ice cream freezer. Her young arms just weren't strong enough to turn the handle for very long, especially towards the end when the ice cream was setting up. Lemon's job that particular day would be to keep me from finding my presents, dirtying my new party dress, or sticking my finger in my birthday cake for a quick sample.

The sun was bright and hot, a typical July day in southeast Kansas. Papa had just purchased new electric fans and they were placed strategically around the large dining room of our apartment over the lumberyard. I wanted to have a swimming party at the Verdigris River, but Momma quickly nixed that idea as in July the water level was low and the water moccasins were in abundance. There had also been a tragic death in July the year before and twin brothers, only nine years old, had drowned and it took days to recover their bodies. This was still too fresh in Momma's mind. The river took its share of human beings annually with its deceptive calm summer water's, only to be taken under by an invisible current and become lodged on the limb of a submerged tree branch. The swimming party was definitely not a good idea.

The children began arriving at the designated time and Lemon placed their gifts on the sideboard in the dining room. Lavender bunting hung in scalloped shapes and was tied with dark blue ribbons all across the room. Many of the presents had the same colors and there was one with pressed violets glued to the wrapping paper in a random pattern that I especially liked. It was pretty the way the mothers of my young guests tried to include the tiny purple flowers that were my trademark in their decorating.

The fresh squeezed lemonade was brought to the dining room from the large, oak icebox in the kitchen and glasses were filled. The children were already thirsty due to the humidity of the day, and little suntanned arms reached eagerly for their cool drink. Everyone was on their best behavior and dressed in their finest party clothes. Maude Read, whose father had a department store in town, wore a pink dress with a huge white sash, and a matching white bow in her hair. Jessie Kloehr wore black trousers with a small black string tie around his collar. Jessie always loved teasing me because he was older, so when he started the taunts about knowing what Papa got me for my birthday, I was as prepared as any newly eight-year-old female child. I begged for more information.

"I can't tell you what it is 'cause I don't want a whippin', but I know what it is!"

He said this in a singsong manner that nearly drove me mad until I managed to distract myself the way Momma had taught me that "young ladies" do in situations such as these.

I quickly walked over to join my friends who had gathered around the gift table. My best friend in the whole world was Sophie Gabler, so I sought her out first and complimented her on her very pretty dress with matching hair ribbon. Sophie lived just a few blocks away, so we got to spend lots of time together and were very close.

Momma soon set up the games and we began to play. There were rings for tossing, handkerchiefs for blindfolds to play pin-the-tail-on-the-donkey, and small tin toy prizes for everyone. Momma didn't particularly like the competitiveness of games, in general, and had told Papa when she was making birthday preparations that everyone would receive a prize as she wanted no hurt feelings at my party.

I opened presents, and we had our sandwiches, cake and ice cream. We were all around the table, wiping our chins like polite, well-taught, little children, when papa entered the room. It was time for my surprise! I could hardly contain my excitement. Jessie Kloehr was grinning from ear to ear as papa made the announcement for all of us to, "Follow Me!" In follow-the-leader style, we formed a line, and giggling and whispering to one another, followed my Papa. We went out the front door of the apartment, through the hall, down the stairs, and out the side door of the lumberyard. We walked around the side of the building to the front of the huge store.

There standing in the street was one of papa's employees, holding the reins to the most beautiful black and white pinto pony I had ever seen. On his back was a shiny black saddle with matching bridle.

"Oh, Papa, what a beautiful pony! And the saddle too. But, Papa, it's a boy's saddle. Does that mean I can ride like you?" I bubbled over.

"Of course you can. You are an excellent rider."

"I had that saddle made for you by Mr. Kloehr, Violet."

"Papa, it's all so wonderful! Can I ride her now?"

"Yes, sweetheart. And every day for a while as she's a little plump. Lil Paint needs someone to love her and take care of her."

Violet

"Lil Paint? What an adorable name. Oh, Papa, yes, I'll take wonderful care of her, I promise!"

All the children lined up for their turn to ride Lil Paint. Patiently, they stood on the boardwalk. When it was their turn to ride, each was given a straw hat to protect his head from the hot sun. Papa was always such a thorough man. We were then led around the parking lot of the lumberyard, papa holding the reins.

After we all had our turn on Lil Paint, it was time for the party to conclude. The children were loaded up in our family buggy to be delivered back home. Everyone was exhausted from the heat, the party food, and the excitement. They waved their good-byes to me with happy, but tired little hands as they pulled away from the lumberyard. The party had been a huge success.

Papa turned to me after everyone had left. "Violet, come sit on Lil' Paint and let Uncle Al take a picture of you." Uncle Al was papa's brother. He was a photographer in Independence. His name was actually Silas Allen Brown, but preferred to be called Al, like my father, who preferred to be called W.P. Papa was named after his father, William, but didn't like anyone to call him Will, except Momma. She's the only one I ever heard call him by that name.

That night as I lay in my bed I felt to be the luckiest girl in Coffeyville, Kansas. Certainly, the most loved, I reasoned. I didn't know any other seven-year-old girls in town with a pony of their own.

Lil Paint, I love you...was my mantra as I fell into a contented sleep, dreaming of riding Lil Paint over the Kansas countryside.

Chapter IV

It was an ordinary summer day in 1892, a day like any other in Southeast Kansas, hot, dry, and windy, when Papa walked out the back door of our lumberyard at 7th and Walnut Street, and discovered what he thought to be natural gas. Right in our own back yard! The excitement it generated spread through the town quickly. Natural gas was still a mystery to most, but my father knew the potential of what it could provide to our town and our own financial future. Many of the town leaders felt that natural gas wasn't safe and were against the idea of gas wells being further developed. Papa argued that he had studied the manufacturing of this raw material and it could be perfectly safe if drilled, piped and regulated properly. He was adamant that natural gas was a necessity to the growth of our town from a small Indian trading town to a large industrialized city.

My father, W.P. Brown, would prove to everyone how important natural gas would be to the future of Coffeyville. His first two wells barely paid for themselves, and the two partners who had signed on with him and invested their own capital, were beginning to waver and lose faith in the project.

One night at supper, he confided in Momma that he wasn't sure if he should continue with the operation. It was costing a lot of money and the last two holes drilled had been dry. Momma, who had money of her own, told him she thought he should try one more time and she wanted to invest her money. Momma had faith in everything Papa did, and hated seeing him so distraught over what he thought would make Coffeyville into the town of their dreams. She convinced him to invest her capital and try one more time. They hit the jackpot.

The brick plants started coming to Coffeyville, the glass plants, and a pottery plant, all for the service being provided by Papa with this new exciting natural gas. W.P. Brown had proven to the townspeople that with proper care of the gas wells they didn't need to fear explosions associated with natural gas. Coffeyville began to grow in leaps and bounds, and my parents became very wealthy.

But what happened in the fall of 1892, made Coffeyville famous all over the world. The Dalton brothers planned a bank robbery in their own hometown. It all happened right downtown, just down the street from where we lived.

I had just finished my breakfast that morning and Lemon was fastening up the back of my dress when I heard Papa coming up the stairs to the apartment, his steps hard and fast. Simultaneously, I heard gunshots and shouting. Papa came hurtling into the apartment and ran directly to his gun cabinet, throwing open the doors, and belting on his holster with the Colt .45 tucked inside. Momma came running in from the kitchen.

"What in the world? Will, what's going on? Are you fighting with someone, again?" She asked in an exasperated voice. She had heard the shots as well. My Papa was notorious for his out-spoken nature and had been in more than one disagreement with town leaders.

"The Daltons are robbing the banks, Nannie. I've got to get out there and help." With that said, he ran past her and out the door.

Momma and I ran to the window and looked out to see what was happening. There were men running past the lumberyard toward the other end of the street where the Condon Bank and the 1st National Banks were located. Yelling for me to stay indoors, Momma ran out the door after papa. I was terrified. Both of my parents were outside where the shooting was going on. I chased after her. When I reached the bottom of the stairs on the west side of the lumberyard, I could see Momma running across the street. There were many people running in my direction and I heard one man shout to another, "Mr. Brown's been shot! Mr. Brown's been killed!"

I could hear Momma screaming as she ran, calling my Papa's name over and over. I ran as fast as I could, calling for Momma to wait for me. She heard, somehow, and turned back, grabbing me up in her arms before she continued into the alley. We could see a pile of lumber. On top of it, was my Papa, alive and shooting toward the east end of the alley. Bullets were flying in every direction.

Papa spotted us at the same time we saw him, and yelled at us to "Get back. Get on the ground and stay there!" Papa's voice sounded afraid and that made me even more frightened than before. A man grabbed us from behind and dragged us back a few feet, shoving us down into a doorway.

"Oh, my God, has she been shot?" The man was pointing at me and I looked down to see if I had been wounded. My feet were bleeding, soaking the skirt of my mother's dress.

"Will," Momma screamed, "Violet's been hurt. We have to get her to Dr. Well's."

I could hear a horse screaming and men yelling above the roar of the guns. Then, as quickly as it had all begun, the firing stopped. Papa ran to us and took me from Momma's arms. He held me to his chest, trying to shield the sights from my gaze. Everyone was shouting. I could hear people moaning and the sounds of running feet. The air was filled with the smell of gunpowder. Moving quickly down the alley to the exterior staircase on Slosson's Drug Store, he carried me up to Dr. Well's office, rushed me into a small room and placed me on an examining table.

Outside the room I could hear Dr. Well's speaking in a loud voice from the top of the stairwell to the people down below in the alley. People were shouting from the bottom of the stairs. "Bring him back out, Doc. We're lynching him here and now! Give him to us."

"Go on home now," he said. "He's only a boy, and he's half dead. Get on out of here and go home." He turned to come back into the office, and was heard to mutter, "Who ever heard of one of my patient's getting well anyway!"

I heard the door close behind him and heard him speak in quick, authoritative tones. We soon realized they had brought one of the outlaws up to Dr. Well's office. Papa looked through the door of the exam room I had been placed in and into the doorway of the one across from it. There lay Emmett Dalton, the youngest of the Dalton brothers, and just like the doctor had said, he was only half alive. His body was a mass of blood, his skin already swelling and bruising. Papa looked over at Momma.

"It's Emmett Dalton," he said, "Doesn't look like he's going to make it."

Papa had done business with the Dalton boys for years. They came to the lumberyard frequently for supplies and Papa had been friends with all of them. He had even let Bob Dalton, the oldest brother; take me for a ride in the new carriage he had purchased from Papa. They were very likable men. Papa looked so confused.

"How could those boys have gone so bad," Papa spoke, in a whisper.

It wasn't long before Dr. Well's came into the room to see about me.

"Little Miss Violet, what in the world has happened to you?" he said in his grandfatherly voice.

"The rocks were so sharp, Doc," I replied.

"I'll say they were. You've got cuts all over your feet. Let me see what I can do to make you feel better." With that he bandaged my feet and then gave Papa and Momma instructions on my care.

Then he hurried into the room across the hall to attend to Emmett Dalton.

As we left Dr. Well's office I could see nothing but carnage in the street below. Animals lay dead that had gotten in the way of the gunfire. I had never seen death before, but I recognized it for what it was.

"You take Violet on home now, Nannie," Papa said. "I've got work to do here."

Momma settled me onto the sofa in the living room of the apartment, and hurried over to the window. We could hear the sounds of movement in the lumberyard below. Momma watched as the men hauled boards across the street and down the alley -- boards that would be used to place the dead outlaws on; their pictures to be taken, souvenirs to be had.

The next morning Momma and I were out front when we saw Mr. Lang and Mr. Lape, the undertakers, bringing black varnished coffins out to be loaded on a wagon, heading for the jail where the bodies of the outlaws had been left overnight. Those four black shiny boxes robbed me of sleep for a fortnight.

They took the bodies of the outlaws to be buried at Elmwood Cemetery. The rail they had tied their horses to, in what was now referred to as "Death Alley," was placed permanently over their graves. Papa told me it was so they couldn't get out.

People came from miles away to see the town where the outlaws had made an unheard of raid on two banks. An "X" marked the spot where the outlaws and the innocent citizens of Coffeyville fell. So many lives lost in such a short time.

Papa's friend, Mr. Kloehr, was acknowledged for killing Bob and Grat Dalton, and wounding Emmett. Mr. Kloehr had no other choice as he watched so many of his friends being shot and killed. When I was older, papa told me John Kloehr confided in him that he had trouble sleeping and horrible dreams after the raid, and felt intense remorse over having shot and killed Bob Dalton, as they had known each other and been friends for most of their lives.

As I lay in bed a few nights later, I listened to my parents as they talked in hushed voices from the living room.

"They buried them face down, Nannie."

"But why," Momma asked with dismay. "That's not a very Christian thing to do."

"They did it as a sign of disrespect," he answered.

"I don't want to talk about this nightmare anymore, Papa." Momma said in a low tone.

It was that very night that I began to feel the love my parents had for each other. I could hear my Papa talking in a low soothing voice in order to calm Momma, giving her reassurance that everything would be all right and that he would never let anyone harm his family. She had been so scared, and my Papa had been so brave.

Emmett Dalton, only a teenaged boy, survived the twenty-three bullet wounds he received during the raid. He stood trial and was given a life sentence at the State Penitentiary in Lansing. He lived his life in pain from the wounds that never quite healed. He wrote a book while incarcerated, which I read. The doctor who saved him, Dr. Wells, became his friend and they kept in touch writing letters and exchanging Christmas gifts until Dr. Well's death.

1892 was one of the best and one of the worst years in Coffeyville history. Loved ones had been lost and the town was grief stricken. No one felt as safe as they had before. The men that survived the raid and had been wounded were permanently disfigured and suffered from their disabilities the rest of their lives.

I still bear the scars on my feet from the rocks in the street.

It is said that time heals all wounds, but I don't think anyone was ever truly able to leave behind the day the Dalton brothers rode into our town and changed our history forever.

Chapter V

My Momma gave birth to Willie in July, 1894. He was a strong healthy baby and everything seemed to be fine. Momma and Papa had been worried and short-tempered throughout the pregnancy, I guess out of fear that Momma would lose this baby too. He arrived on a hot summer day, and I remember the whole town celebrated when they learned of his safe arrival. The townsfolk had felt so bad for Momma when she lost the other baby, so they had been her biggest supporters right up to her confinement. Momma was a quiet and fiercely private woman, and when the ladies in town passed us on the street, as we were taking "our air," they would enquire politely as to how Momma was feeling. Momma always replied "I'm fine, just fine," then smile down at me with what I always thought of as her "secret smile," as if to say to me, "Everything will be all right this time, won't it, Violet."

And it was. Willie thrived, grew, and was loved by all who knew him. He had the face of a cherub with rosy cheeks, blue eyes, and golden curls. His sturdy little legs were always going just as fast as they could take him. He was bright and inquisitive and into everything. I adored him. I loved being an older sister, and would help Momma and Lemon with his care, always feeling so proud and grown-up to get to be a part of it all. After Willie arrived, there was a renewed sense of purpose in our household above the lumberyard, and Momma and Papa seemed truly happy for the first time. Papa's business was growing by leaps and bounds. His discovery of natural gas out behind the lumberyard launched his career in a whole new direction, and Papa was always very busy. Momma would remind him every so often about how she felt we needed a real home with a yard and trees, because the downtown was becoming quite industrialized. There were several gas wells in the downtown area, and beautiful buildings being built on all sides of us. The streets were paved with bricks, as were the sidewalks. The bricks came from Coffeyville's brick plants. The town was growing at an unbelievable rate of speed.

One night as Momma was preparing Willie and me for bed, she was about to burst with excitement about something. Finally, she said, "Children, I've some wonderful news to tell you. We're going to have our own home soon. You'll have trees to climb, grass to play in, and horses to ride. Papa is going to build us our house!"

This wasn't to be just any house; this was going to be a mansion. Papa owned five hundred acres of prime farmland south of the city that had been a working farm and included a large herd of cattle. The mansion would sit at the highest point of the land so that we could look out over the lush green fields and trees. Kansas is not the flat grassland state that it's reputed to be. That's only out on the western edge. We had beautiful hills, trees and lakes. Our land stretched all the way to the Verdigris River, which was an important transportation route.

Papa and Momma had met with their friend, the much-admired architect, Stanford White, in New York, shortly after Momma had lost the baby. The subject of a home had been tossed about, but Momma was very depressed, at that time, and Papa was trying to get her involved in the planning. Now they were in mutual agreement about what they wanted the house to look like and who they wanted to design it. Stanford White had quite the reputation in New York as he had studied in Europe and then worked his way into a partnership with the much-respected firm of C.F. McKim and W.R. Mead.

My parents had been impressed with his designs for the beautiful buildings in New York City, including the Madison Square Presbyterian Church, the New York Herald Building, the Washington Arch, Century Club and Madison Square Garden. Mr. White lived in a fabulous penthouse apartment in Madison Square Garden.

Our mansion was designed to be a home-like livable house with sixteen rooms; all large and light-filled with plenty of windows to make the most of the surrounding view of the countryside. The finest mahogany, birds-eye maple and oak from our lumberyard would be used for the doorways, floors, stairway and window frames. I loved the oak stairway with shortened risers for a gentle ascent, and the bay window on the landing ushered in the soft north light. The walls were to be twenty-inches thick, constructed of double rows of brick separated by air spaces through which heat could travel from the gas furnace to the eight fireplaces throughout the house, all of which would be different in design. Coffeyville bricks were sold all over the world by this time and hundreds of thousands of bricks were shipped out every month.

Stanford White would also design an Inglenook, similar to one he designed for his friend, Louis Comfort Tiffany, in New York. The chandelier in the dining room was to be designed, signed and hung by Mr. Tiffany himself, who would create the gorgeous leaded glass window in the front entryway as well. This main entrance door would face the west as to allow in the most beautiful of sunsets.

Papa wanted to bring in Italian artisans to hand paint designs on the walls. He had seen such canvas covered walls in Europe and in mansions here in America. My bedroom, of course, was to be hand-painted with a violet pattern, with a matching wool rug.

My parents wanted to grow grapevines in an Italian garden that would lie to the south of our new home. The house plans called for the south lawn to slope down to a beautiful goldfish pond, with terraces, gardens, and an arbor supported by large columns with marble lintels.

The layout of the second floor of the mansion included five bedrooms and three full baths. The third floor of the mansion would be a huge ballroom. Our house would also be one of the first houses of its kind to have a full basement under it, with butler's quarters, a laundry room, heating system and a walk-in icebox and storage area. Everything strategically placed to allow for the best light, the best view, and the most comfort possible.

The furniture for the house would come from Sloan's of New York and Marshall Field's of Chicago. Our house would be made from the finest of everything money could buy. Papa spared nothing in designing the house to Momma's specifications. It would take years to complete the house, but when it was through, nothing in the surrounding area for miles and miles would hold a candle to our home, the Brown Mansion.

Years later, I learned that Stanford White had been shot and killed in 1906, by a jealous husband whose wife had confessed to having an affair with Mr. White. As Evelyn Nesbitt and her husband Harry Kendall Thaw were dining at the Madison Square Roof Garden Restaurant, Evelyn pointed out Mr. White to her husband, who simply rose from his seat at the table, strode over to Mr. White's table, and fired three bullets into his head. His short but illustrious career as an architect who built beautiful buildings and neoclassical southern country mansions came to an abrupt end.

Chapter VI

As the house was in the process of being designed, my parents decided that I should receive a more formal education, as I was almost a teenager. Momma and I traveled by train to Topeka to look over the school that had been recommended as the best school for girls in the state, the College of the Sisters of Bethany, an Episcopal boarding school for girls. Once Momma was satisfied that the school was a place where I would be properly trained to become a lady, I was enrolled and preparations were made for me to start the new school term. Although I hated to leave all the excitement of the construction of the mansion, I couldn't help but be thrilled at the opportunity to go to such a fine school as the Sisters of Bethany. Momma assured me I could come home at every opportunity and she promised to keep me informed as to every detail that went on in my absence.

I settled into school life and even began to make new friends. I enjoyed my classes and did well. Our family always loved to read, and I read everything I could find. Life couldn't have been going any better for us.

That would soon change.

On a cold, dreary day in November, 1898, I received an urgent message which stated that Willie had suddenly become deathly ill. I was to be taken to the train station by the headmistress, Miss Annie Hooley, and sent home immediately. I knew something must be terribly wrong with Willie for Momma and Papa to send for me. I prayed all the way home that he was all right. He was the light of all our lives and I couldn't imagine life without him. He was so full of spirit and vitality. I prayed, and I prayed as I stared out the window at the passing countryside taking me closer and closer to home.

Lemon was waiting for me on the platform when the train pulled into the station at Coffeyville. I could see her tears from where I sat by the window. My head fell to my chest and sobs arose from the very depths of my soul. I knew something was terribly wrong with my baby brother.

The conductor escorted me off the train, and Lemon reached for my hand as I stepped onto the platform. With tears in her eyes and a shaky voice, she related to me that Willie had become desperately ill with pneumonia, and the doctors had done everything they could, but early that morning he had slipped away to be with the angels. She held me close in her strong arms all the way home in the carriage, never once taking her gaze off me, stroking my hair, and telling me over and over again that she was there for me, and that I could get though this tragedy because I was strong and that I must be brave for my Momma and Papa.

My baby brother, Willie, was laid to rest in Elmwood Cemetery the next day. His little coffin was covered in flowers and there were floral designs carved into the wood. He was only four years old.

My parents and I left for Ohio that very day to be with my Momma's family, the Kilgores. We didn't come back for a month. I have hardly any memory of that visit, what we did, what I ate, or if I did. I remember only the sorrow, the deep and all-consuming sorrow over Willie being taken so quickly, without warning from our lives forever.

After we returned from Ohio, I was put on the train and sent back to boarding school. Momma feared I had missed too much in my absence and would fall behind if she kept me with her any longer. Education was of the utmost importance to my parents. With a heavy heart, I returned, determined to make the most of my education and to make my parents proud of me.

Before long, I was back in the routine of school. There were days when I would feel ashamed of myself for having, momentarily, forgotten the unhappiness of home, and I would pray to be forgiven for my shortcomings. The fact was, I was very happy to be back with my friends and I loved the day-to-day structure that school provided.

At school, I shared a room with Lena Murdock, who came from Eldorado, Kansas, a small town not far from Wichita. Lena's family was in the newspaper publishing business. We both enjoyed reading and made very good grades in our Literature class. We got on famously. I met girls from all walks of life while at school. There were the two sisters who boarded across the hall. Sandra and Deborah Kogard, each as different from the other as night is from day. Sandra was small, petite, bookish and soft-spoken, and Deborah stood tall, gregarious, and always ready for fun and games. They were from Frontenac, Kansas, the daughters of hardworking parents who had been informed by more than one helpful neighbor, that if you wanted a great education for your children, you sent them to boarding school.

Then, there was Clara O'Casey, the daughter of a preacher, who was absolutely the most daring girl of all. She'd take any dare and not only accomplish it, but couldn't wait for the next one. We often entertained ourselves in this manner when let loose for an afternoon or during the evenings when we didn't have to study. When Clara and Deborah teamed up, which they did often, being of like personalities, we would delight in their antics. The time they decided that a puddle of molasses in front of Miss Hooley's apartment doorway would make for some giggles, only ended up having Miss Hooley step in the molasses, become stuck and then sprain her ankle as she fell sideways. We were all questioned in Reverend Millspaugh's office, and I'm sure the guilty knowledge of who actually committed the offense was written all over my face.

Clara later decided since she had never experienced Halloween, as her parents didn't particularly approve of this so called "holiday," she would risk the chance of her parents' wrath to come home with me for a Halloween experience in Coffeyville. I always loved the fall season, and Halloween in particular. Celebrations were in abundance in the fall in Coffeyville. The moon was referred to as a "Harvest Moon," in accordance with the celebration of the summer crops all having been harvested, and the hard-laboring farmers now able to rest. There was a harvest parade and the mood around town was festive.

Well, Clara came home with me on the train from Topeka to Coffeyville one Friday afternoon in October. Her parents thought she was coming home with me to attend a birthday party for one of my friends. I was very nervous that Clara's mother would find out that Clara had fibbed to her, but I was the only one who worried. Clara reveled in it. We went to the annual town party after the parade, and there were decorations everywhere, all the favorite fall foods like pumpkin pie, pecan pie, roasted pecans that had fallen from the trees at the end of summer, pork and beef being roasted on open pit barbeques. The sights, the smells, the sounds! That night we bobbed for apples with the younger children, played games of hide and seek, and tricked-or-treated the downtown merchants who stayed open late for this particular activity.

Oh, it was fun. The bright orange harvest moon, full and round as a perfect circle, hung in the sky above our heads the whole evening. Not once did Clara worry about deceiving her parents. I'll have to say, it did put a bit of a pall over my festivities, as I was consumed with worry that we would be found out. I didn't particularly care for being part of anymore of Clara's conspiracies, so I didn't invite her home for any more celebrations that her parents wouldn't approve of.

I was a very blessed young lady to have friends at boarding school and friends at home in Coffeyville. When I was home on break from school, Momma always made me attend the Embroidery Club. I didn't actually fancy myself the embroidery type, but I was informed that all young ladies must learn the fine art of embroidery, crochet, and the like. It always irritated me greatly when we would travel back East to Ohio to see my grandparents, and I would be teased about living in Kansas. Coffeyville was every bit as cultured as any city in Ohio. Didn't they realize that everyone who came West was formerly from the East? In fact, Momma felt my social skills and polite manners were better polished than any of my Ohio cousins. Or, at least, that's what she told me to make it sting a little less when I was teased.

We had all the secret societies that everyone else had for the time, and I'm sure some of them were not the kind of societies that doctors shared with their patients, or lawyers shared with their clients. These were very "secret" societies. There was one particular group of women in town called the 13 C.C. Club. They were girls who worked in the same office, or taught school, and they always celebrated the

Fridays of the month that fell on the 13th. Supposedly, there wasn't one among them who was superstitious. How odd.

Embroidery club met every other Saturday afternoon, and I was expected to attend if I wasn't away at school. Mrs. Truby and Mrs. Lang patiently went about teaching us this fine art. Of course, being of an age when young girls are quite giggly and high-strung, so to speak, sitting quietly and patiently was quite a task. There we would be, the cousins, Catherine Chapman and Frances Read, Marguerite Upham, Florence Cubine, Jessie Perkins, Frances Lape, and my best friend, Sophie Gabler, all bright smiles and happy little personalities, making the embroidery club into a time for social interaction and catching up. There would be tea and cookies halfway through the meeting. All the mothers took turns bringing treats, and I would feel such pride when it was Momma's turn to bring the sweets. I always tried my best to learn the stitches like the satin stitch, the lazy daisy, the cross-stitch, whatever particular stitch we were working on that week. Some weeks were easier than others simply because I enjoyed the time with my good friends. I missed them while I was away at school, so I cherished our time together.

As my third year of school drew to a close, I eagerly anticipated returning home as I had worried about Momma and Papa incessantly since Willie's death that cold fall day. She was so quiet when I would go home for weekend visits. Her letters to me at school always assured me they were fine and doing well, but I knew that as much as I missed Willie in our lives, their suffering must be unbearable.

Chapter VII

I came home for summer vacation in 1899 looking forward to time off from school and enjoying my friends from home. I had been home but a few days when Momma and Papa planned a picnic at Horseshoe Bend on the river. People in town loved to go there to enjoy the breeze off the river, have picnics, and fish.

The picnic basket was packed in the buggy, along with blankets for sitting on the grass, and off we went. Since I had arrived home the week before, the house had been quiet. It still felt sad to be home, and have Willie not there, his absence still hurt so much. Momma and Papa tried putting on gay faces, but I could feel their sorrow and emptiness. I did everything I could to make up for his loss by trying extra hard to be engaging and entertaining, but Momma remained quiet. She would smile at me and try to be pleasant, but her smile wasn't convincing.

I spread our blanket on the grass, and sat on the riverbank while Momma laid out the food. Lemon had packed cold fried chicken, buttered bread, fresh ears of corn-on-the-cob, deviled eggs, and apple pie. We ate, at least, Papa and I, until we were stuffed.

After lunch, Papa suggested he and I take a walk along the river's edge and skip some stones so Momma could rest for a bit. She had looked so pale and drawn during lunch, and barely ate a bite, that Papa suggested she take a nap. We stayed down at the river's edge for a time and then I grew impatient to be back with Momma. Papa told me not to worry about her, that she was fine, but I had long ago learned the fine art of worrying, and by the age of fourteen, had mastered it quite well where my Momma was concerned.

As we arrived back at the picnic site, Momma was just rousing from her rest and was sitting up on the blanket and straightening her hair. As we sat down next to her, she looked at me with the most earnest and serious eyes, and I felt my stomach sink.

"What is it, Momma?" I asked, trying not to let my anxiety show.

"My precious Violet," Momma said, "You are such a worrier. Why do you think that something is wrong?"

"You look so serious, Momma" I replied. "The look on your face frightens me."

"There's nothing to be afraid of, Violet," Papa joined in. "Your Momma has something she wants to share with you, and I think she's a little lost about how to say it."

"What is it, Momma?"

"I don't know quite how to tell you this, Darling. I guess the best thing to do is just say it…it looks as if we're going to have another baby."

"What? I don't understand."

"I'm expecting, Violet. It looks like the baby should be here at the end of the year."

"But, Momma, I really didn't think there'd ever be…"

"I know Violet. We didn't either. Miracles happen I guess and we need to consider this as such. I'm not a young woman anymore, Honey; I'm almost thirty-nine years old. I don't quite know what to make of this myself. We're just going to have to work together and hope for the best."

"Your Momma is going to need your help more than ever, Violet," Papa implored.

"Don't worry either one of you," I said, "I'm sure everything will be fine." Although, inside, all I could think was. *Oh no*! *How can we go through this again?*

The Kansas summer passed, hot as ever, and nothing untoward came to pass. Finally, the blessed cool of fall arrived. Momma had bouts of fatigue and napped every afternoon, but other than that, her color was good and she had started to gain some much-needed weight.

It was time for me to go back to school, but I hesitated to leave Momma. I begged Papa to let me stay home that fall and not return to school until I knew Momma and the baby were going to be all right, but he assured me everything would be fine and I was not to worry. I had an education to think about, he reminded me. Education or not, I did not want to go. I pleaded with Lemon to come up with some idea to help me, as Momma was no help at all. But even she thought it would be best if I went back to school. Lemon promised she would do everything in her power to make sure Momma took care of herself, and, of course, Papa was roaring like a lion from dawn to dusk running the household like an ogre in his zeal to meet Momma's every want and need.

My Momma was not a difficult person at all, but she expected her house to be run efficiently and she expected her staff to know their jobs and do them just right. She had gotten so weary of trying to train help that recently, she had asked Lemon to take charge of the house workers. Momma relied on Lemon, and so did Papa. By this time, Lemon had married a wonderful man by the name of Seth Jacobs and they had a little home on East 1st Street. I had never seen Lemon happier.

When I saw that all the wheedling and whining in the world would do no good, I finally became resigned to going back to the Sisters of Bethany for my 9th grade year. Lemon assured me that with one weekend visit per month and Thanksgiving and Christmas breaks in a couple of months, the time would just fly. I continued to worry about Momma, even though she did look so much better and said she felt well. But Papa constantly yelled all over the house about how everyone should do their jobs and keep things quiet for Momma. (Of course, he made more noise than anyone!) Still, I couldn't help being a little anxious.

I overheard more than one conversation between Momma and Papa when they thought they were alone about how nothing could possibly go wrong this time; that God was giving them another chance at happiness, and other sentiments along those lines. I would go to bed on those nights praying to God to please not take another precious baby from our family. My little brother Willie had been such an energetic, happy little fellow, and always wore a mischievous grin on his precious face. Papa had even taught him to sit upon Lil Paint's back, still and straight, while Papa would lead them around. Such a beautiful child he had been. We couldn't bear another loss.

Once I arrived back at school I settled happily into a familiar routine. Everything seemed promising for the days to come, and I vowed I wouldn't think a single bad thought. That year, Indian summer was particularly beautiful and as the brilliantly colored leaves of red, yellow, and orange fell from the trees, my worries fell away too. Fall had always been a favorite time of the year for me so, I worked hard at school and tried to focus on all the good things that were to come with the New Year. Things were going to be different this time…I could feel it.

Donald Kilgore Brown was born on December 13, 1899. He entered the world crying, healthy, with good color, and his prognosis was excellent. All our expectations had been met and exceeded. Momma and Papa were happy beyond belief. I finally felt as if our lives would become as normal as all the other families in town.

Lemon had her first child as well, right before Momma had Donald. She had a healthy baby boy she named Grant, after her father. She helped take care of Momma through her pregnancy while all the time she was expecting herself. She didn't tell any of us about her pregnancy for the longest time, because she was so concerned about Momma. When we finally heard the news, Papa scolded her, and told her she was being completely silly, and then went right to town to talk to Seth, Lemon's husband, who was a well-known and talented carpenter. In his meeting with Seth he explained that he wanted a cradle made and wanted it crafted of the finest hardwoods and a specific design. Seth drew a picture of what he thought Papa wanted, showed it to him, and Papa agreed it was perfect.

It was made of cherry wood with roses carved into the headboard and the footboard. Seth carved a scroll caught among the roses and leaves, and on it he carefully carved the date, 1899. The sides were of turned spindles set about three inches apart. About eighteen inches in height, it had rockers of about the same width, to make it very stable and allow it to be rocked by foot.

It took Seth three weeks of working everyday on the cradle and when it was done he sent word to Papa that it was completed. Papa went to Seth's shop that very day, paid him what they had agreed upon, and then had one of Seth's helpers deliver the cradle to Seth and Lemon's house. Seth had no idea that the cradle he had worked on for three weeks was to be for his own child. When Lemon returned home from work that day the cradle was waiting in their living room and she laughed and cried as she ran all the way to Seth's shop to share the wonderful news.

It was a story that everyone told over and over through the years.

My Papa, W.P. Brown, was a very generous and loving man, and when he liked you he treated you like one of his own family. Lemon and Seth were like family to us and we were all so very happy for them.

Things were definitely looking up.

Chapter VIII

There was much excitement among the girls at school as the end of the 1902 school year approached. We were to have our annual spring dance. I was seventeen years old and hadn't had a lot of exposure to the opposite sex. There had been a couple of school dances with the boys from St. John's School over the past three years. We had the snowball dance right before Christmas and then in the spring we had the daffodil dance before school dismissed for the summer.

But, in my sophomore year the snowball dance had to be cancelled due to an extremely intense winter storm. St. John's School was the military academy for young men in Salina, Kansas. The Sisters and Reverend Millspaugh, the president and rector of both schools, believed it was necessary to teach us how to behave in social situations, and had taught us what they thought was sufficient to learn.

I'm sure the boys found it every bit as entertaining when the headmaster, Mr. Barber, was trying his best to teach them how to lead in ballroom dancing, as we did when Sisters Ursula and Angela were teaching us. We were taught how far apart to stand from each other, the proper movement of our feet, and of course, all the proper manners at the refreshment table.

We all looked forward to these dances, as it was our opportunity for, hopefully, some kind of romantic and exciting encounter. Actually, in all honesty, I was a little afraid of the boys and the idea of the dances caused a certain amount of anxiety and nausea. I don't know what exactly I was afraid of, but I was apprehensive all the same. I pretended that I looked forward to the whole event as much as the rest of my friends and always hid my fears about the whole mysterious situation.

The daffodil dance finally rolled around. I found myself to be quite self-conscious about dancing for some reason that I didn't quite understand, and as I looked about the room at all my friends dancing they didn't seem the least bit disturbed by any of it, as a matter of fact, they seemed to be quite happy.

The only emotion I truly felt when the dance was over was absolute relief that I didn't have to pretend I was having such a wonderful time anymore. That's not to say that I didn't have any fun, I certainly did, but there was also much anxiety associated with the dance that I was relieved when it was over. I always felt all my friends were way ahead of me in the romance department.

By the end of the coming summer, I would find that to be the furthest thing from the truth.

I was to meet a young man who would change my life.

I took the familiar train-ride home that May and arrived in Coffeyville to find much activity taking place. Lemon met me at the station as usual and filled me in on all the latest gossip as we drove to the carriage house we had moved into while the mansion was in the process of being built.

So much had been going on since I had last been home. Lemon chattered away about my friends and their families and all the latest Coffeyville news. She was always "in the know" since her mother, Minnie, took in laundry for the more prominent families in town. As in all small towns everything that went on inside the four walls of other houses was always much more titillating than the happenings in our own. Minnie would arrive at their homes to gather up their laundry and of course would have to "catch up" with the domestic help of that particular house. It was all perfectly natural.

Lemon had been keeping me up on what other families were doing since I was just a youngster.

It felt so good to be home. Everything was in full bloom and the air smelled sweet with the fragrance of lilac bushes, iris beds, honeysuckle and roses. The whole town had been drenched in a rain bucket of spring time.

I could see the activity surrounding the carriage house when we were still a half a block away. There were men of all sizes and shapes carrying cartons and loading them onto wagons.

As we drove up, Momma came out the front door with Donald in her arms and had the most wonderful expression on her face when she saw me. It made my heart leap to see her so happy. She had put on weight and the circles that had been under her eyes in the years since Willie had passed away were finally gone. It had been a good decision to move out to the country and get away from the noise of downtown.

So much had been accomplished since I had last been home at Easter. The foundations had been poured and were "seasoning," as Papa called it. There would be workmen at the mansion for years to come: carpenters, brick masons, plasterers, and other workers. It was so exciting to watch our dream mansion, our "palace" being built.

In the carriage house, I found the walls were painted, carpets had been laid, and beautiful draperies already hung on the windows. My bedroom faced the river and I could see the green water of the Verdigris flowing south at a brisk pace toward Indian Territory. It was a lovely view.

Trees surrounded the carriage house and everything was green and new and fresh. There were no businesses with people bustling around. In fact, there were no noises at all, only the sounds of birds singing joyfully from their nests a welcome home melody just for me.

As I stood there looking at the view from my bedroom window, Papa walked up behind me so quietly and softly I didn't even know he was there until he began to speak.

"I've worked all my life for this, Violet," he said, "and this building is nothing compared to our mansion when it's finished. At times I've felt the Almighty has been way too harsh with me, and other times far too generous. I've experienced a lot of good and a lot of pain. Maybe it's all over now and nothing but good will grace our lives."

Papa had left home sooner than most young men, because his own father had been so hard and abusive, and he had been out in the world ever since forging a way on his own. No one deserved this beautiful palace more than my papa did.

I don't remember saying a word as I stood there looking at that view in front of me. I never even turned around. I just stood there with my papa's big strong hands on my shoulders and I simply placed my hands on his. He had shared with me at that moment the deepest feelings in his heart, and knowing that he trusted me enough to open himself to me in that way is something I've never forgotten. I knew my father didn't consider me a little girl any longer to talk to me in such a fashion and the pride I felt in being his daughter was overwhelming.

He turned around and left the room as silently as he had entered it.

That night we had supper on a small porch overlooking the Verdigris River and talked about our summer, and the mansion. Momma had candles on the table, as it was definitely a celebration. The girls in the kitchen had worked all day and had prepared roast duck with all the trimmings, even a special pudding. Lemon had even stayed late to help with the meal in order for everything to be perfect on our first night.

Momma told her to get on home to her own family more than once; but she was adamant about making our special evening one we would never forget. We were all so happy as we talked about the future. Even now, I can smell that roast duck, hear the birds chirping away, feel the dampness of the night, and bask in the warmth of my family . . . It is etched into my memory and is as fresh to me today as it was then.

That spring night as I lay in bed the sounds of the country were all around me. There was a hoot owl in the big pine by the new stables, and I felt as if he was welcoming me with his soothing sounds. The crickets were humming that tune that is theirs alone, and there was the steady strum of a bullfrog coming from the pond just a short distance away.

What a wonderful way to fall asleep, I remember thinking.

Early the next morning I got out of bed and dressed and went to Donald's room. He wasn't three years old, yet, but I figured he was ready for his first real adventure. I dressed him quickly and we quietly left the house.

I saddled up a horse in the stable and off we went. I was an experienced equestrian by then as Papa had made sure of that when I was still very young. Women were supposed to ride sidesaddle, but I rode astride, like my father.

I lifted Donald on first and climbed up after him. I wanted to get down to my favorite place by the river and watch the sunrise with him. He was such a wonderful little boy, already full of mischief and personality, even at such an early age.

We topped the last small hill and there, before us spread the river. It was full with the spring rains and was out of its banks. The current was strong and swift. We sat there on the horse in absolute silence as the sun rose up over the hill on the other side of the river. Even as young as he was, Donald knew he was experiencing something special. He sat still and straight before me on that horse, barely breathing, as we watched the sun come up together.

That was a special moment in both of our lives. With all that I know now, I am so thankful that I did that.

In June, Momma hosted a party to celebrate my upcoming birthday and every prominent family in town was invited. There would be guests from all over the county, Wichita, Kansas City, and even our family from Ohio would be coming. It was the talk of the town, probably the talk of the state! Everyone was so excited to see W.P. and Nannie K.'s farm, and get a close-up look at the building of our mansion. It was quite the social event of the summer.

It was at this party that I met my good friend, Lena Murdock's, cousin, Roland Percival Murdock, son of Roland Percival Murdock, Sr., publisher of the *Wichita Eagle* newspaper. It was that evening that I would realize what the girls at school had already been feeling about boys for the last year or more.

Papa ordered his workers to lay thick planks of lumber over the foundations of the mansion. Along the sides of the dance floor were uprights supporting strings of Japanese lanterns. Even the moon was cooperative and that night a full moon lent its light to my evening

Everyone was dressed in their finest summer attire. The ladies had been preparing for this day for at least a month, and you could tell by their brand new shoes, dresses, hats and gloves. The men were dressed to the nines as well.

Momma and I had gone to every store on the Plaza in downtown Kansas City until we found what I thought to be just the right gown.

It was in Marshall Field's that I found it and Momma agreed that it would be perfect for the party. It had a full skirt of mauve silk embroidered at the hem with designs of the same shade. The snug bodice was plum colored velvet. Light yellow gauze draperies caught about the bodice with bouquets of flowers that fell as a sash on the skirt. The sleeves were small folds of pleated mauve and yellow silk. It was the most beautiful gown I had ever seen. Of course, I had to have matching shoes, so I found some satin party slippers with hand turned soles, a French heel, and strap buttoning across the instep. As soon as we returned to Coffeyville, Momma took them downtown to be dyed plum to match my dress.

Momma's gown was stunning as well, and we made sure it would coordinate well with mine for those moments during the party when we would be standing close together. Momma thought it would be in very poor taste for a mother and daughter to clash. She found a dress in blue chiffon that was covered in lace and had a deep blue velvet waistband. The lace sleeves were short and over the entire dress was a sprinkling of delicate sapphire colored beads.

Of course, Momma's dress took a little longer to purchase since she never could buy anything that wasn't altered to fit her small frame. We were even lucky enough to find her a pair of size 4 ½ satin slippers just like mine, which she had dyed the soft blue color of her dress.

The guests continued to arrive and the noise level began to increase. Lena stood next to me in the receiving line. She had come down to Coffeyville to visit me and attend the party.

From where I stood by the steps leading up to the dance floor, I could see a man walking in the garden among Momma's roses, a solitary, young man. He was dressed as finely as any man I'd ever seen. He had a drink in one hand and was slowly sipping it as he gazed about him. He was exceptionally good looking with dark blond hair worn in the latest fashion. He seemed very sophisticated to me and completely out of place in a farming community.

Excusing myself from Lena, I found myself walking toward him.

"Hello," he said.

"Hello," I found myself meekly answering.

"Beautiful evening, isn't it?"

"Oh, my yes, just beautiful."

"Were you watching me?" he asked.

"Excuse me?" I felt myself growing faint.

"Just now, while I was out admiring the roses, were you watching me?"

"Why...well, why in the world would I be staring at someone in the garden?" I asked. "I think I was raised better than that. Of course, I wasn't staring at you."

Violet

"Well, if you were I certainly didn't mind," he teased.

I could feel my face growing hotter by the minute with what I was sure was a bright red flush. I couldn't believe he had known I was watching him. It was about that moment that I heard voices and steps behind me. Papa was with a man I had never seen before.

"Well, I see you two kids have already met," Papa boomed.

"Violet, this is Roland P. Murdock, Sr., a friend of mine from Wichita, and Roland's father," he continued.

"Pleased to meet you, Mr. Murdock," I replied.

"Just as I'm pleased to meet you, young lady," Mr. Murdock smiled and reached out to touch my hand.

"I see you've already made the acquaintance of my son, here."

"Well…yes," we both awkwardly replied.

"Well, carry on you two," Papa called over his shoulder, as the two of them started toward the garden. "R.P., Sr., and I have things to discuss. The dancing starts soon, so don't run off."

"So, you're Violet Brown?" Roland said. "My cousin Lena speaks very highly of you. I guess she forgot to mention how very beautiful you are."

At that comment I began to laugh as I could see he was trying to make me forget about the earlier awkwardness.

"What's that supposed to mean?" I giggled.

"It means, my father told me on the way here that I would be meeting W.P.'s daughter this evening, but I didn't expect her to be as stunning as you are."

"Oh, my, you are a charmer. My father has warned me about young men like you."

What an unexpected surprise this had turned out to be. He had the most beautiful eyes I had ever looked into. The color was a shade of green and brown as to be fairly mixed together to form a hazel hue I had never before seen. He was taller than me by three or four inches; his age I couldn't judge, though he seemed older and more mature somehow. My thoughts had run away with me and all of a sudden I realized that a moment had passed. Now, I was staring at him for a second time!

"Let me formally introduce myself. I am Roland Percival Mudock, and I am very pleased to make your acquaintance." With this he bowed slightly from the waist, and as he did his hair fell down over one eye, and as he reached to brush it back into place, I felt butterflies in my stomach.

"I'm very happy to meet you, Roland. As you already know, I'm Violet Brown," and I grinned. I had never felt this kind of giddiness before. What in the world was wrong with me? Was this the "it" everyone had talked about at school? Was this the feeling girls got when they talked to a boy with perfect hair and beautiful eyes - butterflies in their stomachs? I couldn't have been more stunned to find myself in such a situation. I had been so sure that this sort of thing was never going to happen to me. I had felt so far behind all my friends at school.

"Let's go get something to drink," I offered.

"Will you dance with me when the music starts?" Roland asked.

"We'll see," I answered teasingly.

The rest of the evening passed in a blur. I moved among the guests and socialized like I had been taught to do, but kept finding myself looking around the room for Roland. He had definitely made an impression on me. He was quick and bright and certainly knew how to make me laugh. He had asked me to dance twice and it was wonderful. I still found myself to be anxious and queasy about the whole dancing affair, but this was different. I was nervous, but hoped that he would ask me to dance, again. He had asked some of my friends to dance as well during the course of the evening, and they seemed as entranced with him, as I was. I would definitely have to speak with Sophie and the rest of my friends tomorrow and see what they had thought of him.

When the party drew to a close, Roland came up to me and said, "I have so enjoyed meeting you, Violet. I hope we have the chance to meet again, soon."

After everyone had left and we were climbing the stairs to bed, Momma asked me if I had enjoyed the evening. I told her it couldn't have been better, I couldn't have had more fun, and by the expression on my face, and the dreaminess in my eyes, she knew I was referring to the young man from Wichita, the newspaper publisher's son. I couldn't help but notice the rather worried look she had in her eyes, but I was in too much of a swoon to care at the moment. Nothing or no one was going to spoil the wonderful feeling I had inside. Momma had always been such a worrier.

She doesn't have a thing to be worried about, I thought. At that particular moment in my life, I couldn't have been happier.

For the remainder of the summer I daydreamed about Roland Murdock. I replayed our short conversations over and over again in my mind. I discussed him thoroughly with my best friends, Sophie, and the girls from the embroidery club. We had all remained close and would become even closer as the years went by. They had all been in complete agreement that Roland Murdock was simply a dream come true and encouraged my infatuation, thinking he would make quite a nice catch.

I knew Sophie wasn't interested in him and, actually, this really pleased me. She was completely taken by John McCreary, a young man whose father was a Civil War veteran. John was to follow in his father's footsteps and become a lawyer and hopefully a state senator, as well. Every boy I had ever liked when we were younger always liked Sophie instead of me. It's a wonder I liked her at all, but there was always something about Sophie that tugged at my heart, and made me want her happiness almost more than my own. Her father was so very strict that he didn't even allow her to leave the house very much at all.

Valentine Gabler was the President of the Sunflower Glass Company and a very respected figure around town. Sophie had been named after her mother, Sophia, and was the youngest of a very large family. Momma and Papa had always liked all my friends, but I had noticed from time to time, over the years, the disturbing glances they would exchange when Sophie's name was mentioned. Even Lemon would become noticeably quieter, it seemed to me, when I would say something about Sophie.

Not too many years later I would understand the disturbing glances and the silence. I would discover the terrible secret that was Sophie Gabler's life.

Summer passed quickly and my senior year at Bethany awaited me.

Chapter IX

My graduation from Bethany was in the spring of 1904. Momma and Papa came up on the train for the ceremony. I felt such pride for them to see me in my cap and gown, and found myself watching them in the audience as I waited for my turn to receive my diploma.

My friends and I had packed all our things the night before, but instead of the usual giggling, gossiping, and the girl-talk, we were all quiet, reflective, somber. We knew our lives were taking a turn, and that some of us might never see each other again. Of course, we had made all the promises that people make, in good faith, but the reality was we lived in different directions all over the state of Kansas and the chances were slim of our ever being able to revitalize our friendships. We had grown-up together, and now that we were grown, it was time to go our separate ways and out into the world.

It was a sad parting for all of us, but our time together at Bethany was over.

My graduation present was a surprise, my parents informed me, and would only say that it wasn't something I could unwrap and open. But, no matter how I begged and pleaded, neither one would say a word; only grin at each other and shake their heads as they kissed me goodbye. They went on home ahead of me so I could stay for the last festivities of the day. Momma never liked to be away from Donald for any lengthy stays, and they had come up to Topeka the night before. Momma kept saying she "had to get ready," whatever that meant.

During my last trip home from school on the train, I felt very nostalgic. I had always looked so forward to the future and the prospect of growing up. But, now, as the train drew closer and closer to my home in Coffeyville, it was becoming real and the very thought of leaving my school and my friends for the last time and "growing up" became quite unsettling.

What was I going to do with myself? Momma and Papa had talked with me about this over the Christmas break and we had discussed several different things, but nothing seemed quite right. I could work for Papa, do the books and such, and that sounded fine, but at the same time I couldn't help but feel there was something much more exciting I could be doing now that I was all grown up.

I looked out the window of the train as I crossed the familiar countryside. The farmland was green and lush from the spring rains. I had always enjoyed the train ride from Topeka to Coffeyville as the train wound its way through the gently sloping hills. I sensed a transformation about to take place as I changed from high school student into my next role in life; what exactly that role would be remained to be seen.

As usual, Lemon met me at the station. She looked so pretty and smart in her best summer dress and hat.

"Miss Violet, you look like you grew another inch since Christmas vacation!" She exclaimed, smiling and happy.

"Oh, Lemon, don't say that, I don't want to grow any taller," I replied.

"Oh you," Lemon scolded, "I've told you time and again to be proud you took after your papa. Just you wait until we get to the house and see what your parents have in store for you…what a surprise it is!"

"What is it Lemon? I don't think I can wait another minute to know."

"It'll be worth the wait, just never you mind. Patience is a virtue all young women have to learn."

"Oh all right," I said with a pout. I knew better than to try to get any more out of her. When Lemon decided she wasn't going to tell you something, you might as well accept it.

As we approached the long drive to the house, I could see the amazing progress on the house since last I'd been home at Easter. You could tell just how massive the house would be now that the walls were going up all around. It was so exciting to see the progress each time I would come home. It had taken over a year just for the basement to be dug.

We pulled up to the house among a flurry of activity. Trunks and suitcases were being loaded onto wagons, and Momma was busily directing everyone with all their different tasks.

She ran to me as I got down from the carriage and was laughing and talking and hugging me all at the same time.

"Momma, what's going on?" I begged.

"Violet honey, get ready. It's time for your big surprise."

"What is it Momma, please!"

"We're going away for a month," Papa laughed, as he ran up from behind and lifted me into the air. "We're taking you to the most wonderful summer place there is…we're going to Maine!"

This news was too good to be true – a trip to the seashore. I couldn't wait. It had been years since we had visited the east coast. I had wanted to go to Maine and had talked about it often. I'm not sure if it was the scenery, the weather, or something less tangible, but I couldn't imagine a more wonderful place to experience.

All the way out to Maine we talked about our summer plans. Papa had rented a house in Machias as a surprise for the family. At the party the past summer he had learned that many of the best families were doing this, and far from wanting to be different from the rest of prominent society, he was all for it. He and Momma had decided the sea air would be great for all of us, especially Donald. He had been rather sickly the past six months and looked too pale. The sea air had healing qualities and Mamma was always a little obsessive about our health.

Machias was a seaport town in Northern Maine that was gaining popularity as a summer retreat. Papa had found a small cottage right on the coast through a real estate company over the telephone. He described what the real estate agent had told him about it, and his excitement was evident as he told me about the house and the land surrounding it. The ocean was right out the front door, he said, and the fishing and wildlife was reported to be superb. I hadn't seen Papa so excited about anything in years.

Momma and Papa had become quite friendly with the Murdock's over the past year, he explained to me, and they had a home there. Momma really liked Louise Murdock, who was Lena's aunt, and Roland Jr's mother. Mrs. Murdock had quite an interest in interior decorating and had made suggestions about window coverings and fabrics for the mansion, which had impressed Momma.

All I could think of from the moment Papa mentioned the name Murdock was their handsome son and the way he made me feel when I met him at the party. I still couldn't understand why he had made such an impression on me, but he had. The more Papa talked about the house and the seashore and all we would do there, the more excited we all became. It sounded like heaven and we couldn't wait to get there.

The trip on the train took three days, but we finally arrived. It was early evening when we stepped from the train for the short ride to the seashore. We went through the little town of Machias and I was breathless with its picturesque beauty. The quaint storefronts were all painted a different color and I loved the town instantly. We passed the town square with a small gazebo in the middle that was surrounded by the most beautiful flowering bushes. Momma told me they were called shadbush, and the sweet scented white flowers were the first sign of spring. Papa laughed, and said, "Not only do they smell good, but their wood is used to make fishing rods."

We passed by a church that was painted the most brilliant white I had ever seen and the steeple went further up into the sky than any of our churches back in Kansas. The closer we got to the ocean the more we began to notice the seagulls swooping and diving over us causing Donald endless giggling, he was so excited.

We topped a small hill and there it was. The house sat on the point of what the locals referred to as Little Machias. It was a small box-shaped little cottage with faded gray paint; all the windows had shutters with little faded, deep green evergreen bushes carved on them. We thought it was adorable and we hadn't even seen the side that faced the ocean yet. As we all unloaded from the car and stepped forward to check out the rest of the house, it became noticeably quiet. We were in total awe of everything around us. We could hear the sound of tree frogs nearby and a red-winged blackbird flew right past us in a hurry to get home for the night.

And just beyond the house, past the sandy beach, there before us in all its glory was the majestic Atlantic Ocean.

I had never seen anything so beautiful. The sun was just beginning to set, the hypnotic roar of the waves filled the twilight. I was hooked. I couldn't wait to collect my first beautiful seashells.

By the end of the first week at the summerhouse we were all totally infatuated with the ocean and ocean-life. There was a rhythm to life at the seaside that everyone followed instinctively. Donald happily played by the seashore for hours at a time and Momma would have to plead with him to come in and eat. Usually, she just gave in and took something down to him. He built one sandcastle after another. My, he was such a gifted boy. He built huge houses with terraces all around the side, tractor engines, and big barns with silos.

I quickly made friends with some girls I met in town on a shopping trip with Momma. Isn't it interesting how all teenagers gravitate just naturally to one another in unfamiliar places. My new friends were three sisters who had been coming to Machias since they were little girls. Louise, Maxine and Betty Williams became my dearest friends. They introduced me to everyone that I *should* meet, and made sure I was invited to all the summer parties and occasions.

We hadn't been in Machias two weeks when I was invited to my very first beach party. The weather was beautiful that day and families dotted the beach all up and down the bay. The shore was busy with colorful umbrellas, lawn chairs on the sand, and buckets and shovels. Life here was great. We lay in the sun, waded in the ocean; it was far too cold to actually swim, and walked the beach looking for seashells.

And then I saw him. That very afternoon I saw him on the
beach. . . Roland Murdock. He was with a group of other young men, but I picked him out immediately. I had been looking for any sign of him since we arrived, but wouldn't admit it out loud to my new friends. They knew a little about Roland because I told them about the party the summer before, but they didn't know about the butterflies I would get in my stomach at the thought of seeing him here.

As my friends and I started down the beach toward them, Louise, Maxine and Betty chattered excitedly because they knew the young men, but I grew more anxious by the second. The girls stopped and began to visit with them while I stood there toward the back of the group, wishing the beach would open up and swallow me, I was so nervous. Why I wanted to disappear I had no idea. I had been waiting for this encounter for the entire two weeks we had been here. Now here he was and I was feeling nauseous enough I honestly thought I might be sick.

The girls were asking all the young men if they had made my acquaintance yet. Then he stepped forward grinning that impossible grin, and said, "Well, well, Miss Violet, so we meet again." I hoped I wasn't smiling too ridiculously big because I could see that he was full of himself already, but I couldn't help it, I was overjoyed to see him again. My stomach sank to somewhere around my knees and I was speechless.

It seemed as though everyone was talking all at once and I vaguely heard someone saying, (most likely Louise, she was the most talkative,) that there would be a clambake this very evening and everyone must surely come.

I took special pains with my dress that evening. Momma helped me with my hair and Papa and Donald kept asking me what the special occasion was. Momma would shush them and then go back to reminding me about everything I should remember to do and everything I shouldn't do. I joked with her that I couldn't believe there was even such a thing as "beach etiquette."

Nannie K., my Momma, was always a firm believer in manners and how to carry one's self in a group of people. She would even correct Papa and how she got away with that was always a mystery, but somehow he found it amusing. Very few people amused my Papa.

Louise, Betty and Maxine arrived at the cottage for me around 7 P.M. They were as dressed and primped as I was. We all walked down to Jasper Beach where the clambake was to take place. This beach was beautiful as it had a most unusual deposit of jasper pebbles. Long before we arrived, we could smell the huge black cauldron filled with bubbling seaweed, clams and lobsters. The aroma wafted down the beach and our mouths watered just smelling it.

There were young people everywhere and the mood was festive and gay. This was so different from anything I had ever experienced where I grew up. There was a city band playing in a small park not far away from the beach and the music carried down to the water. There were small sailboats tied to the dock. Young boys fished from it with their bare legs dangling back and forth.

I was glad I had dressed warmly as there was a steady chilled breeze off the ocean. At this time of year back home the last thing we ever needed to worry about was having a warm sweater nearby for comfort.

All the young people surrounded the bonfire that had been built and were talking together as we approached. Roland was already there by the fire. Sitting with a local girl, he saw me, excused himself, and came to stand next to me.

"I'm so glad you came, Violet," his voice was deep and smooth as honey.

"I wouldn't have missed it," I replied. My heart had begun to pound and I was having a very private internal conflict with myself that he would not have that effect on me tonight. *What was it about him?*

Supper was announced and we were called over to the bubbling lobster and clam pot. Roland walked over with us and as our food was dished out and handed to us he asked if it would be all right if he dined with me. Luckily, there were other young men wanting to eat with Louise, Betty and Maxine as well, so I didn't feel as nervous.

We went to the table with the drinks on it and each picked up a cup of lemonade and then sat down on the pilings provided for us to use as seats. Roland leaned over and conspiratorially whispered, "I have a little something here in my pocket that will make that lemonade taste like heaven. It'll warm you up, too."

My heart jumped up and down in my chest.

"What is it?"

"Something that's imported from Canada. You'll love it."

"Well, give me a little to see if I like it."

"I guarantee you will. I haven't met anyone yet who didn't."

He poured some of the amber colored liquid into my lemonade cup. I took a small sip and decided that it wasn't bad. The only thing I noticed at all was the way my throat felt a little too warm as I swallowed it.

"Well, what do you think?"

"I think I like it…it's hard to tell. I didn't really taste anything but the lemonade."

He winked as he said, "You want some more then?"

"Well…"

"Come on Violet, you've got to learn to live a little. You're considered a grown-up now that you've graduated high school, might as well enjoy the benefits."

"I guess you're right."

The thoughts were rushing through my head throughout this short conversation. All the formal training I'd had from school and from my Momma. What was appropriate and what wasn't. I glanced over at my friends, and every one of them looked to be having a great time. I made up my mind at that moment that it was time for me to do what I wanted and not what I thought someone else would think I should do, or what might be expected of me.

"Another nip then, Miss Violet?"

"Oh all right, I guess a little won't hurt anything."

After supper, there was a dance on the enclosed dock. We all finished eating about the same time and started to make our way over there. Louise, Betty Maxine and the young men they were with walked up with us and we all stood talking, waiting for the dancing to begin. The girls were whispering fiercely to me about their individual dates, and I found myself to be just as excitedly whispering back. This was something new. Maybe it was that imported Canadian whiskey taking away my apprehensions, but whatever it was I liked it because for the first time I didn't feel absolutely nauseous over a dance. As a matter of fact, I was actually looking forward to it.

"Let's all have a drink before the dancing starts," Roland offered.

He pulled me close to him as we danced, closer than he should have I knew, but I didn't care. It felt like a dream and a dream I didn't want to wake from. I felt as though I was in some kind of trance, and could hear him as if from far away, whispering in my ear…endearments.

Suddenly, it was as if I couldn't catch my breath, and I pulled away from him and started toward the end of the dock where I could feel the breeze blowing in from the sea, cool against my face.

I felt his arms encircle my waist.

"Let's get out of here, Violet," he whispered as he pulled me close to him. "I have a boat tied down at the end of the dock and the fresh air will do you good."

"Yes, that's a good idea," I answered.

He rowed out into the bay and then set the small sail. The wind immediately began to take us out and it felt refreshing on my flushed skin. The dizziness and breathlessness began to pass.

"I don't know what happened back there. I feel so foolish."

"Don't apologize, you aren't used to alcohol."

"Where are we going, Roland?"

"There's an island just across the bay, Seal Island, and it's most beautiful at night. You're going to love it."

It didn't take long and we were there, pulling up onto a sandy shore that was completely lit up with moonlight. He took my hand and helped me from the boat and then turned around and got a small blanket that had been tucked under the seat.

"Here," he said. "Sit and be comfortable and look out across the water." I looked back towards Machias and could see the lights twinkling on the water and the light from the Quoddy Head lighthouse flashing every few seconds. *This is the most beautiful evening of my life*, I thought.

"I've had such a wonderful evening, Roland."

"It's only just begun," he murmured as he pulled me closer to him. He began to kiss me then, slowly, deeply, and I could feel that sense of unreality smothering my senses again. It wasn't a feeling I even dared to fight. It was as if by opening my eyes it would all truly have been a dream, so I didn't. As he began to lower us down onto the blanket, I pushed against his chest in hesitation and he stopped the kiss and gazed longingly into my eyes saying not a word.

It was as if time had stopped.

Finally, he said, "We don't have to do this if you're not ready, Violet."

With my finger against his lips, I murmured, "Shhhh...I don't want to think about if I'm ready or not...I just want to feel..."

I pulled him close to me and kissed him deeper still. I was lost in the sensation and could think of nothing other than this most fascinating mystery termed *lovemaking*...the murmured endearments, the breathlessness of expectancy, the all-consuming emotion of two becoming one. From that moment I knew I was lost to him and a prisoner of the feelings he had inspired.

I knew I was in love with Roland Murdock.

The cool sea breeze on my flushed skin and the sound of the ocean beating against the shore brought me back to my senses. I lay on the blanket very still and watched him from the corner of my eye, in total disbelief of what had just occurred. I could feel hot tears falling one by one. *What have I done?*

Roland lifted my chin and our eyes met. "Are you all right?" he said. "Did I hurt you?" he whispered.

"No, I'm fine," I said with tears in my voice.

"Violet, what is it? Why are you crying?"

"This whole evening has been so wonderful, and you've made me feel so special."

"You act as if being special isn't something you're accustomed to. I find that a little hard to believe. Everyone that knows you adores you."

"Things aren't always what they seem, Roland."

"What do you mean?"

"I mean that my family has been through a lot over the years and it hasn't been easy. I really don't want to talk about this right now. This evening has been so special and now I'm ruining it."

"You haven't ruined anything, my sweet Violet. We better get you home now though. The hour is definitely getting late. I don't relish the thought of W.P. coming looking for you."

"Roland, what happened tonight?"

"What happened tonight?"

"Yes...I don't know...I just feel so confused. Was this *wrong?*"

"Darling, don't worry. Everything's fine. We've had a wonderful evening and now I'm going to get you safely back home."

"Will I see you again Roland?"

"Well, of course you will. Haven't you realized it yet? I'm your Destiny."

I spent less and less time with my friends and more time with Roland. We went to the shops, sailed in his boat, went to parties, and of course, went back to Seal Island. Momma said I was spending too much time with him and I could tell she was worried, but I didn't care. I was in love. Papa, on the other hand, was a little more vocal about his displeasure of my devoting all my time to one young man. He liked Roland and found him to be quite acceptable, but at the same time disliked the whole idea. I rationalized this with the thought that all fathers must go through this and dismissed it. Papa needed to get used to the fact that I was grown up now.

June drew to a close and July was in full swing. We had settled into the routine of life on Machias and all of us were happy. Donald was as brown as a berry and had even put on weight in the six weeks we had been there. Momma and Papa were closer and happier than I had seen them in years. The seashore had been so good for us.

As in all things though, this too would soon come to an end.

There had been trouble back in Kansas with Papa's gas company and he had received three or four telegrams over the past two weeks that there were things he needed to attend to, but it was the news of an approaching hurricane that made him and Momma decide we had better get back home.

Tornadoes in Kansas were bad enough, you could at least seek shelter in a cellar, but a hurricane was something altogether different indeed.

Oh, I didn't want to go home. I was having the time of my life. Roland assured me that he would be going back to Wichita soon after I left because nothing would be the same without me. That made it a little easier to go. I knew I would be seeing him again and that was all that mattered.

Chapter X

July 12, 1904, I awoke to birds singing and the smell of sweetbread baking. Lemon always made sure there were special things to eat on our birthdays. I was turning nineteen today.

I sat up in my bed, stretched and jumped out of bed, eager to start the day. I headed down the hall to the bathroom and, suddenly, out of nowhere, I was so dizzy and nauseated I could barely stand.

I leaned against the wall and waited for this god-awful feeling to pass. After about a minute, it did and I continued on down the hall to the bathroom, went in and walked straight to the sink to splash some cold water on my face. As I was drying my face it happened again. I grabbed hold of the sink to steady myself and as I looked into the mirror I was shocked at how pale and white my face was. It was as if all color had drained from it.

What in the world is happening? Of all days to be sick, not on my birthday! Maybe I just needed to go have something to eat. The dizziness was the worst part, as I had never experienced that sort of sensation before.

I ventured downstairs slowly and Momma, Papa, and Donald were already at table.

"Good morning, dear. Happy Birthday," Momma called as she saw me coming into the room.

"Good morning," I replied, rather weakly.

"Nineteen today, Violet. Lord, how the time has flown," Papa said.

"Happy Birthday, Sister," Donald said, in his sweet sleepy voice.

About that time, Lemon walked in through the door carrying a large platter of cinnamon sweetbread. "Well, good morning to you, Miss Violet, and Happy Birthday. Isn't this just a glorious day?"

"Good morning, Lemon." I replied.

"You all enjoy this cinnamon bread and if you need anything else just holler. I'll bring in the bacon and eggs, shortly."

"Violet, are you feeling all right? You're pale as a ghost this morning." Momma enquired.

"Oh I'm fine, Momma. I just think I need to eat a little something."

"I thought we'd go into town this morning and let you pick something out at Truby's. I told Lemon I'd be going to town. She needs some muslin; so I need to go into Barndollar's and pick that up for her too. Honey, are you listening?"

I was feeling that horrible dizzy feeling again and trying my best to keep anyone else from noticing. I obviously wasn't doing a very good job with my Momma, which wasn't surprising.

"Violet, you do look a little peaked," Papa said worriedly. "Are you sure you're feeling all right?"

"You two are such worriers," I replied. "I'm sure I'm just fine. I think I'm still a little tired from the trip home."

Momma and Papa exchanged worried looks. About that time, Lemon came through the door with the scrambled eggs and bacon on a steaming platter. She placed it directly in front of me on the table.

I felt nausea rise up in me, immediately. *What is going on?* It was starting to worry me.

"I think I'm going to go on back upstairs and take a bath, and get ready to go to town Momma. I'll eat a little something later." I couldn't have cared less at that moment to go pick out jewelry at Truby's. I was feeling desperately sick and all I wanted to do was lie down on my bed and hope that this would quickly pass.

I was no sooner up the stairs and into the bathroom when the retching started. I had eaten nothing, but it continued just the same. I pressed a cold washcloth to my face and the feeling began to recede. I wanted to g lay down. I had gotten into bed and had the cloth pressed against my forehead, when that dizzy, nauseous feeling washed over me again.

I quickly ran to the bathroom and was kneeling in front of the toilet when Momma knocked on the door and came in. I retched and retched while she held my hair back and resoaked the washcloth, holding it to my cheeks to cool them.

I was weak and exhausted when it was over. I sat there on the floor unable to move for fear it would return. Momma was standing there with the oddest look on her face, studying me. "Violet, what in the world...?" she said. Her face showed confusion and worry. "What is going on here? Honey? You're so rarely ever sick, and on your birthday."

A moment passed. A puzzled look came over her face.

"Oh, my God, Violet, does this have anything to do with that Murdock boy?"

"Momma...I...Oh, Momma, I feel so sick."

"Oh, dear Lord," was all she said in reply.

"Let's get you back in bed."

She helped me down the hall on my weak, unsteady legs and tucked me into bed. All the while her face was etched in worry and concern.

"Violet, you need to talk to me, now, and you need to be very honest. How intimate have you been with Roland Murdock?" Momma pleaded.

"Oh, Momma, please...I don't...don't make me..."

"Tell me . . . did you have your monthly in June?"

I couldn't look at her.

"I guess that answers my question."

"Momma, please don't hate me," I pleaded.

"I don't hate you Violet, but I can't help but be disappointed. It scares me to even think about what your father's reaction to this will be."

With that she walked out of the room and quietly closed the door behind her.

I must have fallen asleep because when I opened my eyes again it was after noon. I felt better, but was afraid to get out of bed for fear it would start all over again. Just as I was getting ready to climb out of bed, Momma came through the door.

"I'll be going in to town shortly. I'll go by Dr. Starry's office and make an appointment for you to see him tomorrow afternoon. We'll have your birthday supper at 7 o'clock, and as soon as supper's over, I'll talk to your father."

"Oh Momma, do we have to tell him yet? Maybe we're wrong about this."

"Violet, you've missed your June cycle, you're nauseous and dizzy, there's no doubt in my mind. We'll have Dr. Starry confirm it tomorrow. It will be best to get the news of it to your father over with and get on with what needs to be done next."

"What do you mean...done next?"

"Just let me take care of it. I'll figure it out. You rest for now and I'll see you tonight for supper."

I dressed and went downstairs. On the way through the kitchen I passed Lemon who was making preparations for the night's meal.

"Miss Violet, Honey, you all right? You don't look very happy with it being your birthday and all. I thought you were going shopping with your Momma."

"I'm fine, Lemon. Just not up to a shopping trip. I'm going to go outside for awhile."

"I'll bring you something cool to drink in just a bit, then. How's that sound?"

"I'll be down by the river, Lemon. Thank you."

I headed down to my favorite spot on the riverbank. I watched fish swimming back and forth and could feel the breeze on my face. What would have been typically very enjoyable for me wasn't even a distraction. My thoughts were scattered all over my brain.

Momma hadn't said the word *pregnant* out loud, and I hadn't even thought about a baby when all this started this morning. Could it be? It was definitely possible. I had missed my cycle in June, but had barely thought about it until now. *Oh, my God...a baby. Could this really be happening? A baby! Our baby...Roland's and mine. My heart began to swell and my eyes glistened with tears. This isn't a tragedy. This is a baby. Roland and I love each other. Everything will be all right, I just know it. Of course, this isn't the way it's supposed to happen, but it will all turn out, I know it will.*

What will Roland think though, my thoughts turned dark once again. Marriage had never come up once in our time together. *I know he loves me though. I know he does. He'll be happy about the baby.* No matter how I tried to convince myself of a happy ending, the whole process of thinking it through had thoroughly worn me out and all I wanted to do was go lay down once again.

I'll feel better this evening, I thought. *It's my birthday and what a wonderful gift to receive.*

Somehow I wasn't convincing, even to myself.

Violet

I sat in front of the mirror and brushed my hair. I would put the brush down and then pick it up and start over, anything to keep from having to go down to supper. I had never felt nervous about my own family, before. Finally, there was no putting it off and I left my room and went downstairs. Momma and Papa were coming in the front door and Lemon was calling to Donald from the back door as I walked into the room.

"Well, my beautiful girl, are you hungry this evening? Lemon's made all your favorite things," Papa said joyfully.

"I've been smelling something good all afternoon," I replied.

Momma and I kept exchanging looks and I was sure it had to be obvious to Papa, but he seemed not to notice. I tried to make up my mind to enjoy the evening and worry about everything, later.

"Violet, why don't you go tell Lemon we're ready to sit," Momma said.

"No need, Mrs. Brown, I'm right here, and so is the food. You all just sit yourselves down and we'll proceed with this birthday feast," Lemon said all smiles.

"What have you prepared for us, Lemon?" Papa enquired.

"Well, sir, I have barbecued chicken with my spicy sauce, scalloped potatoes with lots of cheese, just the way Miss Violet likes them, baked beans, corn on the cob, and corn bread hot out of the oven. How's that sound to everybody?"

"That sounds like a birthday supper to me, doesn't it, Honey?" Papa said.

"It sure does, Lemon." I answered. "The house has smelled like good cooking all afternoon."

"Are you guy's going to quit talking about food and just bring it out, Lemon?" Donald asked. We all laughed.

"Sure thing, Mr. Donald."

With that, the girls who worked in the kitchen came through the door with food in both hands and sat it all down before us. It did smell good. I was so thankful that I didn't feel sick like I had that morning. I was actually hungry.

"We have your favorite chocolate cake for dessert, Miss Violet." Lemon offered.

"It sounds wonderful, thank you, Lemon."

"It's my pleasure, Miss Violet, you know that. Now you all go on and eat your supper and enjoy it."

"Thank you, Lemon. Everything looks wonderful," Momma replied.

The conversation throughout supper was the usual with talk of the lumberyard, gas prices, and talk around town. Momma tried extra hard not to let Papa know anything unusual was going on. So far, he seemed unaware. Donald, on the other hand, even at his young age, kept glancing up at me and knitting his eyebrows together in a question mark. He was such a little character and so very intuitive.

"So, did you girls go to Truby's this morning?" Papa asked.

Momma and I exchanged looks and each waited for the other to speak first. Finally, I spoke up and said, "I wasn't feeling very well this morning, Papa, so we decided we would go tomorrow, instead."

"Nannie, you make sure Truby gives you a good deal on whatever you two choose. He owes me one for that lumber I sold him at just over cost last month."

"Of course, he will, Papa." Momma answered.

"You girls sure aren't eating much this evening," Papa observed.

"I think it's the heat," Momma replied.

"Um," I answered.

Lemon brought out the birthday cake. She had outdone herself. The cake was beautiful. I was officially nineteen.

As soon as supper was over I excused myself to go upstairs and as I left the room, Momma and I exchanged one last look. I felt so awful she was doing this for me, but at the same time so very grateful. My Papa and I had always been very close, and I don't know how I would have told him what we suspected to be true.

"Papa, let's sit on the sofa and have a brandy," Nannie K. said.

"That sounds like a good idea."

It wasn't unusual for them to have a drink together after supper, but the tone of Nannie K.'s voice alerted W.P. that something was amiss.

"We need to talk," she answered the question on his face.

"What is it, Nannie?" W.P. asked worriedly.

"I want you to sit down, Will, and listen quietly while I say what I have to say." Nannie spoke as she sat down on the chair opposite him.

"Well, now you're sure acting mysterious. What in the world is going on? You don't have to tell Lemon to fire another girl do you?"

"It's nothing like that."

"Well, what in the world is it? You're starting to worry me."

Nannie K. got back up out of the chair and poured W.P. a glass of his favorite brandy. As she handed him the glass and sat down again she began. "Now, Will, this isn't good, but it isn't the end of the world either…we've been through so much in this family that actually…"

"For God's sake, Nannie, spit it out and get it over with."

"All right then. It's about Violet."

"Violet?"

"Yes. I think she's in trouble, Will. You know how much time she spent with that Murdock boy while we were out East."

As the meaning of what Nannie K. was saying began to sink in, color began to bloom in W.P.'s cheeks. He rose up out of his chair. "Are you telling me that Violet is expecting a child? Is that what you're saying?"

"It hasn't been confirmed yet, but, yes, that's what I'm telling you."

The shattering of the brandy snifter against the fireplace brought Nannie K. up out of her chair.

"Will, calm down. We'll work this out. Please, don't upset yourself."

"Work it out?…work it out?…you're goddamn right we'll work it out! That Murdock boy is going to pay for this, by God! I'll be on the first train out of here in the morning and we'll see how it works out!" With that, he stormed out, yelling for Lemon as he went.

"Lemon?" he roared.

"Yes, sir, what is it, Mr. Brown," Lemon answered as she came rushing from the kitchen.

"I need a bag packed, Lemon, I'll be leaving in the morning." He yelled over his shoulder as he stomped up the stairs.

"Of course, Mr. Brown." Lemon answered as she looked after him.

Oh Lord, she thought. *What is it?*

As she turned to go back to the kitchen she could see Mrs. Brown sitting with her head in her hands, looking for all the world like she'd suffered her worst blow. She quietly walked the long length of the living area and softly asked, "Mrs. Brown, are you all right?"

Nannie K. looked up with tears swimming in her eyes. "Oh, my God, Lemon."

I could hear my father from my bedroom upstairs. I could hear him storming up the stairs and heading down the hallway. I waited for him to come crashing into my room demanding an explanation for the outrageous story my mother had just told him. The door slammed at the other end of the hall. I let out the breath I realized I had been holding since hearing his heavy tread on the stairs.

There was a soft knocking on my door, and I was about to get up when Donald quietly slipped into the room.

"Sister, what's wrong with Papa? Why is he so angry?"

I pulled back the covers and motioned for Donald to climb in next to me. "Don't worry, Sweet One, you know how Papa can get some times. He's probably just having trouble with someone in town." Oh, God, how I hated myself at that moment for lying to him.

"Can I stay in here with you, for awhile, Sister?" Donald pleaded. "Papa's scary when he's loud like that."

"Don't you worry," I soothed as I stroked his soft little blonde head. "Everything will be all right come morning."

I pulled Donald close to me and hummed to him as he fell asleep.

Oh, please, God, I begged. *Please let everything be better in the morning.* With that prayer on my lips I closed my eyes and waited to hear the sound of momma's soft steps on the stairs. I fell asleep feeling as if I had disgraced my parents and myself as well.

Nannie K. quietly opened the door and looked into Violet's room. She could see Donald snuggled up close to his sister and felt her heart cry out with the pain of knowing that everything was about to change, again.

She closed the door and with a heavy sigh, slowly walked to her room at the other end of the hall.

How would all this end?

Chapter XI

Momma received a telegram two days later. It was brief and to the point. Pack our things and come go to St. Louis immediately. The summer home was ready and Papa would meet us at the station there. She was to notify him which train we would be taking.

I had spent most of the past two days in my room and that's where Momma found me. Dr. Starry had confirmed our suspicions and Momma had aged overnight. *This is my fault and I won't ever be able to make it up to her.*

"Violet, you need to get up and start packing, Honey."

"Where are we going, Momma?" I said through tears already forming.

"Well, I know we'd planned on going to the World's Fair this summer, but we really hadn't planned on going for another three weeks. Your father has obviously spoken with Roland's family and they've decided to have the marriage take place there."

"Marriage..." I said hollowly. "Momma, why haven't I heard from Roland? Why hasn't Papa let us know what's happening in Wichita?"

"I don't know, Violet. We just have to trust that your father has everything in hand and do as he says. I'll have Lemon come up and help with your packing."

"Momma, I can't tell you how sorry I am for all of this." I was miserable that I had caused all this hurt.

"Let's not speak of it, Child. We just need to go take care of what needs to be done."

The World's Fair was scheduled to be in St. Louis, Missouri, the summer of 1904. There had been advertising in the papers for months. We had scheduled our trip for August, and Papa had secured a home for the two weeks we had planned on being there. Momma informed the staff at the mansion that we would be going to St. Louis earlier than planned. Lemon was the only one who knew the details. Momma trusted her implicitly and after Lemon had seen her crying, in the library, there was no reason to try to hide the inevitable.

Lemon helped us pack and, loyal devoted person that she was, asked no questions. She just offered her support in her usual loving way; a soft-spoken word of encouragement, a light pat on the back as she finished buttoning my dress, the extra gentleness as she brushed and styled my hair.

She took Momma, Donald and me to the train station that same day. Momma and Lemon stood over in the corner of the platform and spoke for some time, both with anxiety and worry pinching their faces. I'm sure Momma was going over all the instructions for Lemon, the do's and don'ts, while we were gone. She needn't have bothered really; Lemon knew what to do, what not to say. She stood patiently and listened to everything, nodding occasionally. Lemon knew Momma needed to go over everything as a way of calming herself.

We finally boarded the train and waved goodbye to Lemon as she stood on the platform watching us leave.

Momma had wired Papa of our arrival time and he was there waiting when the train pulled in. It was the first time we'd seen each other since the night of my birthday. I was terrified of how he would treat me. Momma could sense my anxiety and reached over and interlaced her fingers in mine and assured me everything would be fine.

As we got off the train, he barely acknowledged either of us, just motioned for us to follow him to the carriage he had nearby. On the way to the house where we would be staying he made polite conversation with Momma and would only glance at me from time to time.

Oh, my God, my father hates me, I thought. I had never felt so miserable. *How in the world would I get through this? Why doesn't he tell us what happened in Wichita?*

I didn't dare ask any questions. I sat there silently and stared out the window of the carriage without any real interest in the unfamiliar scenery we were passing.

We arrived at the gates of a three-story brick home. The uniformed servant opened the gates, greeted us politely, and directed us up to the house. My curiosity about this beautiful home overcame my gloomy thoughts and I looked around with awe. The estate was beautiful. We drove in under a portico and Papa helped us out of the wagon. There were flowers planted everywhere, enthusiastically greeting us with their scent. I looked out over the grounds and noticed the presence of a black wrought iron fence enclosing the yard. We walked toward the back of the house at Papa's direction, and he pointed to a large gazebo in the backyard. "The marriage will take place here," he said with barely concealed anger in his voice.

I could finally stand it no longer and responded, "Papa, must you be so cruel and mean? How can you act as if you hate me?" I sobbed.

"Violet, that's not it at all. I hate to upset you with the details, but let's just say my meeting with the Murdock's did not go as I had hoped."

"Papa, you need to tell me everything that happened," I pleaded.

"No, Violet. I won't do that. I will tell you that there will be a marriage here on the twenty-fourth, and your Momma and I will do everything we can to help you through this, but I have serious misgivings about Roland Murdock and his ability to see you through this time of need."

"She needs to know what she's getting into, W.P. I would rather you spare us the details, but just what exactly happened?" Momma replied tersely.

"Let's go in and get settled a bit, and then I'll tell you all about it."

We went into the house and were shown to our rooms. Papa had said to meet on the screened-in porch in thirty minutes. The porch was on the east side of the home and you could see the gazebo from there. The gardens were gorgeous with color everywhere and in every shade.

Momma and I arrived before Papa, each moving toward matching white wicker rockers, sighing as we sat.

"Momma, whose house is this?"

"It belongs to a business associate of your father's. They summer in Maine, and they graciously offered us the use of the house while they were gone when they learned we would be coming to the World's Fair."

The World's Fair was something I had looked forward to, as well as my family. I had no desire whatsoever to attend the fair now.

Papa and Donald entered the screened-in porch and walked toward us. A servant entered after Papa with a tray filled with glasses and a pitcher of what looked like iced tea and a plate of fresh cookies. He left as quietly as he had entered.

Momma filled the glasses and handed one to each of us. Papa reached for a cookie and ate it unconsciously as he looked out into the backyard. Donald climbed up into papa's lap and was handed a cookie.

"Well, my girls, I won't keep you in suspense, any longer. I met with Roland, Sr. and informed him of what had taken place with his son and Violet. He wasn't too pleased I can tell you that. Of course he didn't want to believe it any more than I did, but he took me at my word. We've known each other long enough for him to know I wouldn't be in his home throwing around accusations if there were any doubts. After we talked for about an hour he sent for his son. When Roland, Jr. saw me there in his father's study he looked as if he wanted to bolt for the door. I told him there was something we needed to discuss and from that point on everything went downhill in a hurry.

"At first he tried to deny the kind of relationship I was implying he'd had with you, Violet. He's spoiled, arrogant and quite undisciplined, I'll tell you that much. I'll have to say his father informed him there would be no unscrupulous behavior in their family and that he expected him to do the gentlemanly thing. After approximately five minutes of what I can only politely describe as *whining* Roland realized he was going to be held responsible for his actions. He's not happy about this, Violet, I'm sorry to say. At no time did he even pretend to act as if he were sorry for the predicament he has put us in. He has agreed to the marriage, however, and as I said earlier, it will take place on the twenty-fourth, which by the way just so happens to be Roland, Jr.'s twentieth birthday."

"Did you get to meet with Louise Murdock, W.P.?" Momma enquired.

"Yes, I did. She is a very sincere and honorable woman. She was quite distressed over the circumstances, as she has had a certain young woman of privilege in mind there in Wichita for her son for some years now. She recovered from the shock of the news quickly enough though and was quite willing to help Roland, Sr. and me make the plans for this union to be carried out."

I was totally speechless as I stared in the direction of the gazebo. Finally, Papa spoke again. "Violet, have you nothing to say about everything I've told you?"

"I don't know what to say, Papa. I wasn't foolish enough to believe Roland would be happy about this, but I didn't think he'd actually try to deny the love we shared. I guess this means he doesn't love me, doesn't it?" I sobbed bitterly.

"Oh, what have I done?"

Momma and Papa looked at each other and then at me, and Momma began to softly cry. Donald climbed down off papa's lap and into hers and wrapped his little arms around her neck.

Papa got out of his chair and came to me, knelt in front of the rocker and took my hands in his. "Honey, we'll get through this, don't you worry. He's just confused right now, just like you are. Men don't take things the way women do. He'll come around, you'll see. How could anyone not love my Violet?"

My big, strong papa, usually so gruff and business-like was trying so hard to be convincing and put my mind at ease while, at the same time, trying the best he could to stifle the fury he felt over the situation I had put myself in. He still was loving me and putting me before all else just like he always had.

I laid my head against the back of the rocker and closed my eyes to the grief. Rocking slowly back and forth, this motion being a time tested method of calming the most despairing of souls. I didn't even try to hide my tears from my parents as they rolled down my cheeks one after the other.

Chapter XII

I awoke to thunder and lightning and a pouring rain. It was my wedding day.

I turned over in the bed and buried my face in the pillow. This was the worst omen of all; rain on one's wedding day.

There was a soft knock on the door and Momma looked in.

"Violet, it's time to get up and start preparing. The Murdock's will be arriving in a few hours time. You need to eat something and then I'll help you dress."

There hadn't been time to shop for a wedding dress, so Momma had decided I should wear the dress I had purchased for my graduation only a few short months before. She had been working for several days sewing beautiful ivory lace around the collar and sleeves, and along the hem. It was a simple dress, but the lace had transformed it. Momma had cried as she sewed the lace into place, remembering her own wedding and how happy everyone had been for her and the new life she would share with the up and coming entrepreneur, W.P. Brown. She had often dreamed of the beautiful wedding she would give her only daughter. Now, she could only accept that things had turned out differently and she would do what she had to do to move forward and not look back.

Sitting by the window, I attempted to eat a piece of dry toast and felt nauseous as I had every morning for the past few weeks. A cup of hot tea sat steaming in front of me and I tried a few sips. The rain continued to pour from the heavens.

There was again a soft knocking at the door, and Papa entered the room. He had a small rectangular velvet box in his hand. He sat down opposite me, extending the box toward me as he sat. "This is from your mother and me," he said, his eyes so earnest and full of love. "Every woman should wear pearls on her wedding day."

In the box was a single strand of pearls, the barest shade of pink. "Papa, they're beautiful," I replied.

"They pale beside you, my precious daughter. No jewel in the world could compare to what you've brought to my life these past nineteen years. Your happiness is everything to me. I want you to remember that, always."

"I love you, Papa. I'm so sorry for hurting you and Momma."

"Shhh. We have to look forward from this moment on. I've brought you up to be brave and strong, don't you ever forget that. There is nothing you could do that would ever change the love I have for you, my firstborn child. We'll get through this, don't you worry. Your mother and I will always be here for you."

There were tears in his eyes and I knew it was hard for him to let me see the pain he felt. He had wanted so much for me. He rose from the chair and turned to leave the room. At the door, he turned back and gave me his familiar wink and then left the room.

It was time to get dressed for my wedding.

The skies cleared around noon. The Murdock's had arrived at precisely 11 A.M., and Momma had come up to tell me. She suggested I stay in my room and advised me that Louise Murdock would be coming up shortly to see me.

"No, Momma. I don't want to see her. I can't."

"You can and you will, Violet. You will start being brave this instant, and don't you for one moment act as though you are ashamed of anything. You must never let the Murdock's, or anyone else, see anything but confidence in your face. You're not the first woman this has happened to and God knows you won't be the last. Louise Murdock will accept this just as I have and be all the better for it. I have already spoken with her and I am confident there will be no outbursts or sentiments displayed; only well wishes for you and her son. In time, we will all grow to accept what's happened, you'll see."

"Yes, Momma, you're absolutely right, of course. I'll try my best to do exactly what you've suggested."

Louise Murdock paid her visit and let me know within moments exactly where she stood on the matter of her son, me, and the marriage that was about to take place. She was polite, but chilly, and gave me the definite impression she thought I had *trapped* him purposely.

The training I had received from my Momma definitely came in handy as I never once let her know she was upsetting me, and I remained soft spoken and polite throughout the entire conversation.

"Everyone's upset right, now," I kept repeating to myself. "Things will get better." Mrs. Murdock would see that her impression of me was completely mistaken.

The ceremony was to take place in the gazebo at 5 P.M. Not once, between 11 A.M. and 5 P.M. did Roland even attempt to come and see me. Momma told me it wasn't appropriate for the bride and groom to see each other before the wedding, so I kept reminding myself of that and trying to convince myself that was the reason he was staying away.

The Justice of the Peace arrived shortly before 5 P.M. Papa, Momma, Donald and I stepped outside and the Murdock's, all three of them, stood waiting in the gazebo. Their faces were frozen and Roland looked like a stranger. He was looking right through me and his face bore the look of an accuser. Papa and Momma stood on each side of me as we processed down the stone path to the gazebo. I felt as though I were being escorted to the guillotine instead of my wedding ceremony.

We took our places and the ceremony began. It began and ended in a blur. The only memory I took with me was the look in Roland's eyes as he faced me and repeated his vows. His eyes were vacant and cold, with no trace of the man with whom I had fallen in love.

Papa and Momma had already informed me that Roland and I would be staying at the Carriage Inn for our honeymoon and the arrangements had been made. We would leave right after the ceremony.

We walked from the backyard and through an arbor gate covered in flowering purple clematis vines to the front of the house. There was a carriage waiting for us. My parents each hugged me, and Louise and Roland Sr. each shook my hand and we were off.

My marriage ceremony had taken less than fifteen minutes.

The carriage pulled beneath the awning of the Carriage Inn. We went into the lobby and Roland asked for the keys to our room. The arrangements had already been made for us to have the honeymoon suite.

We went up in the elevator, the bellboy let us into our room and we were finally alone.

I was exhausted and it showed. There had been little attempt at conversation by either one of us. I was removing my hat when the telephone rang. Roland answered it.

"May I speak to Mrs. Murdock, please?" enquired a voice on the other end of the phone.

"I would assume this person is referring to you," he said sarcastically as he handed me the telephone.

"Hello?" I answered warily.

"Mrs. Murdock? This is Dennis at the front desk. I'm sorry to bother you ma'am, but I just received a phone call from Mrs. Brown, and she wanted me to inform you that Miss Lemon is on her way to the hotel."

"She is?...Oh thank you so much." I hung up the phone and was turning to leave the room when Roland spoke.

"What was that about?"

"Lemon is on her way to the hotel."

"What on earth for?" Roland quipped rudely.

"Momma told me Lemon offered to come up and help me with my clothes and hair and such while we're here this week. We'll surely be going out?" I enquired.

"I suppose," he said sulkily. He moved toward the table in the sitting area where a big basket of fruit had been placed. He plopped down into one of the chairs and bit into a pear.

"I guess I'll go change my clothes and get ready for supper," I said with a false air of everything being all right.

"Yeah, right," Roland replied distractedly.

I took off my wedding gown and slipped into my robe, and was lying on the bed resting when Lemon arrived. Roland answered the door and directed her back to my room. She walked through the door and hugged me tight as I rose to greet her.

"Did everything go all right, Miss Violet?" Lemon asked.

"It's done," is all I replied.

"Well, let's start getting you ready for your first supper as a married woman." Lemon said busily.

Lemon was just starting to brush out my hair when Roland entered the room and asked Lemon to come into the living room suite for a moment. She came back a moment later looking confused and anxious.

"Miss Violet, Mr. Roland just asked me for my key to the suite and then got your key out of your bag. He was talking to himself, mumbling kind of, and all I could make out was 'I need a drink.' Then he walked out the door and locked it behind him. Miss Violet, I'm sorry to have to tell you this, but…he locked us in here."

"Locked us in here?" I asked astonished.

"Oh, honey, I'm so sorry." Lemon said with tears shining in her eyes.

"Why is he doing this to me, Lemon?" I cried.

It was my wedding night and I was locked in the honeymoon suite of the most beautiful hotel in St. Louis. I threw myself down on the bed and cried until there were no more tears left to shed.

Chapter XIII

I lay on the bed facing the wall trying to make some sense of what had just taken place. But, of course, I couldn't.

Lemon sat in the armchair next to the bed. She had been silent for so long that I thought maybe she had left the room. I slowly turned toward the chair, and there she was. Of course she hadn't left me.

"Miss Violet, I've been doing some thinking," Lemon said, getting up as she spoke.

"If I called down to the front desk, they could send a bellboy up with a key, but what excuse could I give?" She wasn't looking to me for a response; she was formulating a plan out loud.

"A key is necessary to get in or out."

Roland Murdock had been so casual. He had asked Lemon for the key to the suite saying that he had misplaced his. Then he had picked up my purse, opened it, removed my key, and just walked out the door. Lemon hadn't grasped what was going on until it was too late.

She was pacing the room, glancing out the windows, trying to console me, and from the looks of it, exhausted from her trip all the way to St. Louis from Coffeyville. "Lemon, you must be so tired, and hungry, too. Quit worrying about me. Have you had anything to eat since you got here?" I asked as I raised myself up into a sitting position on the bed.

Seeing the huge basket of fruit on the dresser, Lemon started toward it and distractedly picked up an apple. She bit into the apple and continued to pace the room. "Miss Violet, why don't you have a piece of fruit, too? It's actually quite sweet. Only thing that's missing is a little cheese." Lemon's eyes began to widen and she turned toward me finger pointing toward the sky.

She'd thought of something!

Rushing to the bathroom, Lemon turned the water on in the tub and poured in some bath salts. She grabbed a towel and the bathrobe hanging on the back of the door, before going to the bed.

"Miss Violet, I have a plan. Here, now, let's get you out of that gown and into this robe. Then I want you to get into the bath tub and let me handle the rest, okay?"

"All right." I was only moving because Lemon was confident and capable. Lemon had taken care of me since I was five years old; she'd do the same now.

Within five minutes, I was in the tub and I could hear Lemon on the phone.

"Room service, please."

"Yes, this is the bridal suite. I'm just drawing the bath for Mrs. Murdock and won't be available to the door. Please bring up some sandwiches, hot tea with milk and sugar, and do you have some good cheeses here?"

The answer was of course, "Yes." And "what kind would you like?"

"Oh, and could you just let yourself in, as I will be busy attending to Mrs. Murdock. Thank you, so much."

As she replaced the phone, she hugged herself in glee. Mr. Roland Murdock wasn't so clever. She had outsmarted him, and he would know it. Maybe when he got the bill he would figure out how she had accomplished it.

She came to the bathroom door and explained what was going to happen, then went back into the bedroom to sit on the bed and wait.

There was a soft knock at the door. Lemon stood and waited quietly. As the key turned in the lock, Lemon moved toward the door.

The waiter rolled in a cart with a teapot inside a tea cozy, and there were three covered dishes, along with the necessary place settings. Lemon waved toward the armchairs by the window.

"Over there, please."

"Oh, thank you, so much. My mistress is very tired and will be so grateful for your prompt service. Wait, wait, a minute." Lemon went to Violet's bag and opened it, removing two dollars from the little purse inside.

"Here, take this. Don't bother to lock the door. I'll be going to my room in a minute and I'll take care of it."

Thanking him repeatedly, she shooed him out into the hall. Closing the door behind her, she leaned against it grinning.

"Are you about ready to get out, Miss Violet? We have a snack waiting for us, complete with tea and apple pie. What do you think?"

Entering the bathroom holding a huge, Turkish towel Lemon waited until I stepped from the tub and began to help me dry myself.

"Let's get you into your robe. That's it."

"Now, would you like to sit in this chair or on the bed?" She gently guided me by the elbow through the bathroom door back into the bedroom.

"I think I'll sit in the chair." I couldn't help but grin just the tiniest bit.

The next hour was surprisingly pleasant. Lemon turned on the radio and we listened to music while we ate. There was a sense of accomplishment in the room. Lemon had turned the tables on Roland Murdock. There was a small measure of satisfaction in that.

After that night, Lemon and I never spoke of my wedding night again. Roland had returned shortly before dawn and slept on the sofa in the living area of the suite. I could smell the liquor a room away where I attempted to sleep. I'm sure Lemon rather wished that Roland had been able to appreciate her ingenuity, but she never said a word.

That next afternoon, Lemon suggested we take in some of the World's Fair. Roland said that he couldn't think of anything more boring than walking miles and miles to see replicas of things and places that he had visited in real life. We went without him.

There were so many buildings, each with the flavor of the country whose exhibit was inside. Entire lakes and giant birdcages had been constructed to show off the flora and fauna of different regions of the world. Many countries sent musicians and dancers to show the culture and arts of their nations.

We went to the Mississippi River to see the ships of many nations and the steamboat races. It wasn't appropriate for a young lady to go alone. Of course, it wasn't appropriate for a bride on her honeymoon to be sightseeing without her groom, either.

I wasn't interested in souvenirs from this trip. They would only be a reminder, I thought, of the misery and confusion I had endured. But, the day we were coming back to the hotel from the river, we passed the window of a shop in which was displayed the most beautiful hat I had ever seen. Lemon convinced me to go in and try it on.

It was a huge swirl of white chiffon, and Lemon said it looked like a beautiful cloud framing my face. It looked so light, so wispy, that a strong wind could destroy it. Somehow white, silk roses were suspended in this glorious cloud, peeking out of the chiffon like perfect accent marks over a foreign word. It had been my bright spot of the day, and it felt good for just a moment, to feel happiness, for whatever small reason.

The honeymoon lasted approximately one week. I barely saw Roland at all. He would come to the suite to change his clothes and then promptly leave.

We never shared a meal, a kiss, or a bed.

He would show up in the wee hours of the morning, fighting to fit his key into the keyhole of the door, muttering and cursing, obviously drunk. He would collapse onto the sofa and stay there until he would awaken and start the whole process, again.

I was totally heartbroken. Lemon pointed out the dark circles under my eyes, my lack of appetite, the depression she could see slowly consuming my days and nights. I had never felt so alone in all my life. When she suggested the two of us go out sightseeing again, I said no.

The last day we were in St. Louis, Roland knocked on my door and asked if he could enter my room.

"Can we talk?" he asked.

"I can't imagine what you could possibly want to talk to me about," I replied.

"I'm sorry, Violet. I've treated you horribly all week, and I'm truly sorry."

I sat up in the bed where I had been napping to pass the time, and quell the continued nausea I experienced every morning.

"You have hardly spoken one word to me all week, you act as if you despise me, and I'm simply supposed to accept your apology. And then what?"

"I've been a callous bastard, I know. I can't even explain the way I've been feeling. This has all just taken me by such surprise and I wasn't prepared for it, I guess. I've completely taken it out on you and I realize now how wrong I've been. I've wasted the whole time we've been here being angry and resentful."

"Can I please take you out to dinner tonight, Violet, and try to make amends for my behavior. Can I make it up to you? Please, Violet?" He pleaded. "We can start all over. I promise from this day forward to do everything in my power to make you happy."

I sat in the bed with the pillow hugged tightly to my chest, tears flowing freely, wanting so much to believe everything that was pouring from his lips. I had spent the better part of a week in total despair and hopelessness. All I could think was *this is my life now*. What else could I do but make the best possible effort I could. I certainly couldn't go home to Coffeyville with things the way they were. That would be far too humiliating, and this experience, so far, had been humiliating enough already.

"All right, Roland. I'll go to dinner with you," I finally answered. *Maybe he does really love me, I* thought to myself.

"Great. I'll make all the arrangements. You just get ready and we'll leave around seven. We'll have a good time, Violet. I promise. I won't disappoint you again."

With that said he flashed me his most enigmatic smile and dashed out the door.

Should I trust this? I thought. *What choice do I have...I love him,* my heart responded.

I called down to Lemon's room and asked her to come up and help me dress.

"Don't worry about a thing, Honey." Lemon soothed, as she brushed my hair. "Men are selfish creatures, but they come to their senses, after a while. Everything's going to work out just fine. You'll see. I've prayed this would all work out and the Good Lord has always come through for us, so you just keep on thinking good thoughts and before you know it, things'll smooth out."

She helped me dress and continued to murmur encouraging thoughts until she almost had me convinced this could actually work. I was still in a very emotionally unstable state as we left for dinner, but I was starting to feel more hopeful with every moment that passed.

Dinner was a success. Roland had flowers delivered to the table and the setting was very romantic. He spent the entire meal catering to my every need. There was a small orchestra and they played music conducive to lifting my spirits. After we finished our meal, he asked me if I felt like dancing. Reluctantly, I complied. As he held me close and made promise after promise, I felt my doubts begin to fade.

We left the restaurant and returned to our room late in the evening. The bed was turned down and there were candles burning all around the suite. I felt apprehension and anxiety begin to well up inside of me. Tears that I thought had all been shed over the past week weren't far from the surface.

"Please let me show you how sorry I am for everything that's happened," he begged as he pulled me into his arms.

As he laid me down on the cool satin sheets of what should have been our honeymoon bed, my thoughts and feelings melting like so much wax in the elegantly tapered candles, I could only tell myself that he was my husband now, and I needed to forgive him and begin to trust him. I gave my heart and soul to him in that moment and knew that I would do everything I could to make this marriage work.

Violet as a toddler

Willie Brown with his nanny; Violet at age 11

Violet and Donald in the pony cart

Violet as a young teenager; Violet and W.P.; W.P. with his brother, Silas

> Coffeyville, Kan
> April 29, 1908
>
> Dear Violet,
> I have been very busy for so long that I could not write to you and Roland. I have been making a farm. My barn and my animals are cut out of paper and pasted on a blue piece of paper. I am also making a book of physiology pictures. I am making an oc- quarium. I had a turtle but he got away from me. I made a wire pen for him. He had a tank of cement to swim

A letter from Donald to Violet, 1908

Donald Kilgore Brown, age 8

Donald's letter to Violet

We have been reading Trimson Cruso and Jack [?] going to make a book of it, that is the picture. It mak[es] a [?] with an overflow on it but they [?] it. I haven't got your basket [?] yet. I had it here a time with my [?] watercolors but did without it. Christmas things. Mr. Hudson and I have been [?] firing old croquet grounds. I have been swimming two times with the Carpenter boys. And when we got out we were hungry. A baby ung- on [?] by some got some cookies. Sam going again this Saturday.

Its old mule called the [?] the river and [?] across but we did [?] till [?] two day. Papa asked Billie Carpenter to come down and swim, but he said, "I can't swim". I made a shirting but it was flour down. Sam [?] going to make another

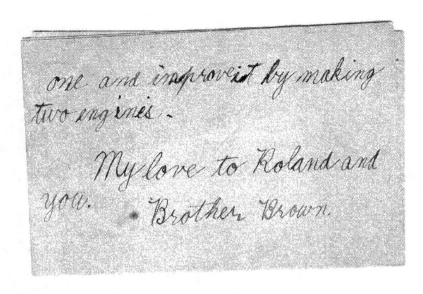

1908 letter p3

Nancy Kilgore Brown (Nannie K.); Violet in Venice

Violet, circa 1904

Violet and Nannie K in the garden

House in Machiasport, Maine

Violet in her late teens

Brown Mansion; Violet circa 1970 (photo by Shane Roeder)

Chapter XIV

We returned to Coffeyville to begin our new life. We would be staying at the Eldridge Hotel in town, which was owned by my father. We had a suite on the third floor that overlooked The Plaza. We decided it would be the best place to stay until we could decide where we wanted to live. Roland was excited to begin his new job and I was ready to start my new life.

Papa had ventured into the newspaper business for a short time a few years earlier as a way to voice his Democratic views and opinions. The paper had been called *The Democrat*. My Papa was a very staunch and devoted Democrat and I had overheard his boisterous, loud discussions with members of the opposite party many times over the course of my childhood. As a matter of fact, it was a much known fact around town that if you were a Republican, Papa automatically disliked you.

For our wedding gift, Papa gave us the newspaper. It was to be called *The Coffeyville Record* and Roland would hold the title of proprietor and business manager. Roland Sr. and Papa had come up with the idea since the newspaper business was in the Murdock blood, and they both felt that Roland, Jr., would be right at home with his new career. Roland, Sr., had assured Papa that his son had the talent and ingenuity to make a success of the paper and that his experience working for him would ensure he was ready for the challenge.

We settled into our new life in Coffeyville. Word had spread around town that we had married in St. Louis and now we were back home. My first call was from Sophie, anxious to know all the details. She couldn't hide her disappointment that I hadn't confided anything to her, but I assured her everything had happened so fast I hadn't had time to confide anything to anyone. She was not going to be satisfied with that answer, and soon we were snuggled up on each end of the sofa in my new living room and I was telling her the whole story. It felt good to have my best friend to tell all my secrets to and felt she was trustworthy to keep the part about the baby to herself until Roland and I decided it was time to let everyone know.

Sophie knew all about keeping secrets. Her father was a very controlling and authoritative man who did not like for his daughters to have any freedom and kept them on a very short leash. He not only didn't approve of her leaving the house much, but every time the subject of the opposite sex was brought up, he quickly reminded his daughters that he had other plans for their lives. Sophie was the youngest of the six daughters, and not one of them had been allowed to date. Her five grown sisters still resided at the family home with their father only allowing them to do alterations and seamstress work that was brought to the house.

Sophie had secretly been seeing John McCreary for some time and the thought of her father finding out could actually bring out goose bumps on her arms and legs. She was terrified of him. The secret would be safe with Sophie until I chose for it to be public knowledge.

Life at the Eldridge House was different than I thought it would be. All I had to look forward to was dinner at night as Roland worked long hours at the paper. I would try to do my embroidery and keep the apartment straightened up, but I was bored. I was used to the structured life of school and summertime had always been a fun time with my friends. I was still having morning sickness and would spend many hours just lying around and waiting for it to pass. Lemon's days were extra busy as she would go to the farm and oversee things there, and then come to the Eldridge to see about me. I could tell that she was really tired. She had children of her own at home, and I'm sure it wasn't easy for her to handle all her different responsibilities. She wasn't one to complain though, and since Momma had asked her to help care for me while I was in this delicate state, she would have never let anyone know she wasn't up to the task.

Momma wanted to have a party for Roland and me. She had been busy planning it from the time she came home from St. Louis. She was just waiting for me to feel better. I finally told her to go ahead and set a date and not to worry about me because I usually felt pretty good in the evening, anyway. She set the date for the middle of August and began to send out invitations.

The day of the party arrived and I spent most of it at the farm. I missed being with my family, and most of all Donald. He was only five years old and really didn't understand why I didn't live at home anymore and why I couldn't take him horseback riding like I had in the past. Momma kept making excuses for me, as he was too young to understand the real reasons. He just knew that he missed his sister taking him riding and was unhappy about it.

Everyone was looking forward to the party and Roland was in an especially good mood as we dressed for the party. He did seem a little anxious but I pretended not to notice as he poured himself another drink.

We arrived early, as instructed by Momma, so we could help greet the guests as they came. It was a beautiful summer evening.

The cicadas were chirruping their summer song, the tree frogs were accompanying them, and there was a steady cooling breeze coming from the northeast, which was not typical for August in Kansas.

People started arriving, one after the other, their carriages pulling up and unloading family after family. Everyone greeted Roland and me with enthusiastic smiles and well wishes. His parents had arrived the night before. They stood behind us in the receiving line. I wasn't the least bit surprised when they had each given me a hug and a kiss. They certainly weren't going to act chilly in front of a room full of people.

Soon, it seemed the room was filled with music, laughter, and the tinkling of glasses. I had stood in the entryway and greeted people for over almost an hour and was starting to get tired. I excused myself and walked to an open window for some fresh air.

I was hit with the strongest feeling of de ja vu. Had it really only been one year since I had met Roland for the first time? *Oh, how I had felt that night, so full of hope and anticipation of the times to come. How much had changed in the year since meeting him. How was it possible that I was a married woman and expectant mother already? My life was just getting started...yet why did I feel so sad, almost a feeling of doom?*

Momma came up to me and touched me lightly on the elbow, saying, "Violet, come on back in now. Papa wants to make a toast to you and Roland."

"To my daughter and my new son-in-law...may they have a lifetime of happiness, health and many children to fill their home." Everyone raised their glasses of champagne and drank to our happiness. Roland was standing next to me with his arm around my waist, smiling his most attractive smile, his face tilted down to mine with a look of total adoration.

If only I could believe it, I thought to myself as I too smiled in acknowledgement of the toast. I was still a little gun-shy after the week in St. Louis, even though Roland had been very congenial since that last night there.

The mood was festive and when the music started Roland and I moved to the center of the floor and began to dance. As he spun me around the floor and held me tight I felt as if nothing could equal this moment. Maybe things would be all right after all. I had begun to think this was an enchanted evening and hoped that it would never end.

The spell was broken on the way home to the Eldridge Hotel.

"Your father has got to be the most outspoken man I've ever met," Roland said.

"What are you talking about?" I asked.

"Well for one thing, his political views are completely biased, and the way he thinks he absolutely runs the town of Coffeyville. What an ego the man has."

"Well, Roland, I really don't think…"

"And what about your mother?…who does she think she is, telling me how I should be taking care of you?"

"She did what?"

"Oh yes, she informed me that you need to be taken out in the fresh air for walks more often, I should be coming home for lunch, and on and on. Your parents are just way too overbearing, Violet."

"I really don't think it's that bad, Roland."

"Well, I do. I'm a grown man and I don't need to be told what to believe as far as politics are concerned, and I certainly don't need to be told how to take care of my own wife."

"My parents are just very protective, that's all."

"Your parents are just too used to having everything their way is what I think."

"I don't think that's fair, Roland."

"Fair? None of this has been fair. I don't see my parents treating you as if you need to be told anything. They would never think of doing anything so crass."

Violet

"Crass? I hardly think my parents are being crass. And, as far as your parents are concerned, your mother made it very plain what she thought of the whole situation on our wedding day, and I'm sure that opinion hasn't changed one bit. How dare you act as if your parents are better than mine, or more refined than mine, for that matter!"

I was absolutely boiling by this point. Roland's tone of voice sounded exactly like a petulant child who wasn't getting his cookies and milk after his nap. He was wound up and getting tighter by the moment.

"I will not have your parents trying to run our lives and you better get used to that, right now" he said in a voice that became louder and louder.

"You're obviously drunk, and I think this conversation has gone far enough," I said with a sigh.

"Oh, now you're going to get dramatic on me, huh? I've just worn you out with my complaints about your parents? Well, as far as I'm concerned, I haven't even started. Ever since your father made the trip to Wichita and demanded I marry you, he's thought he could pull me around like I have a ring through my nose."

"Demanded?" I said on a sudden intake of breath.

"You better believe he demanded. He told me I'd be a dead man by the time the sun set if I didn't do the right thing by marrying you."

I was stunned into silence. It hadn't been Roland's decision to marry me at all. My father had demanded it, and he had simply followed instructions. How could I have fooled myself into thinking he was only disappointed over the way everything had happened? He wasn't just disappointed over the fact we had to get married, he was furious about it. I could hear it in his voice.

We pulled up in front of the hotel and the doorman came and helped me down.

"I'm terribly sorry to have ruined your life, Roland," I said crestfallen.

"Ruined my life? No one or nothing will ever ruin my life, my dear. You might as well understand that right now."

With that he drove off into the night with me standing outside the hotel choking back the tears until I got to the privacy of our suite.

Chapter XV

A few weeks later Momma suggested we move to the farm. She had learned, from Lemon, I suppose, that I was alone most of the time and not doing well emotionally. I had lost weight and spent more and more time in bed. Lemon would come in daily and try to lift my spirits, but it was in vain. She knew that Roland wasn't spending his evenings at home with me and that I was basically alone except for Sophie's visits.

When Roland was home he was drunk and argumentative. He wasn't doing a good job of running the paper either. Papa had made more than one comment about Roland having been seen coming out of the Carey Building, just southwest of the Plaza. The main building was home to Truby's Jewelry and other reputable offices, but the boarding rooms above had the reputation for being able to be rented by the hour. My father was a wise man and had fantastic intuition, so none of my made-up excuses for why Roland could possibly be there went over very well. He could tell things weren't right no matter how hard I tried to pretend they were.

Momma finally convinced me to come back home by using Donald. She knew that would do it. He was usually the only thing that would force me to focus on something other than myself. It was just impossible to continue to feel gloomy in the presence of this special young boy. He was always talking, sketching, building something extraordinary with his blocks, continually in motion. I realized how much I missed him.

I informed Roland I would be moving to the farm and he could either come with me or stay at the hotel. I didn't really care what he did. I was so tired of trying to atone for what had happened.

He left shortly after the conversation, which had become his habit, but then returned a few hours later.

Violet

I awakened to the sound of the key turning in the lock and fear began to inch through my insides. *Oh, no. Why has he come back? What will he do this time?* He usually didn't come back to the hotel until well after midnight. I lay as still as possible pretending to be asleep, but I could feel him coming towards me in the dark.

"Wake up, damn you," he snarled in the darkness.

"Roland, get out of here, please. You're drunk." I begged.

"I'll go when I'm damn good and ready. You listen and you listen well. Nobody tells me what to do or when to do it. You and your family think you're so goddamn high and mighty. I've got news for you. The Murdock's could buy the Brown's three times over. If you think I'm going to just lie down and let your precious Papa walk all over me like he does the rest of the people in this town, you're mistaken. I don't know whose idea it was to move out to that pathetic farm, but I know the reason behind it. It's so that family of yours can watch every move I make, praying for me to mess up, just so they can talk over their nightly brandy about how they were right about me, all along. Are you listening to me, Violet? I see how you look at me, the contempt in your eyes, the disgust. I make you sick, don't I? Don't I?" He was screaming and the arteries were bulging in his throat, his eyes were huge, his mouth an angry bright red slash on his face.

"Get out of that bed right now and look at me when I'm talking to you."

I rose slowly out of the bed, now fully terrified. I had never seen him act like this before.

The minute my feet touched the floor and I was standing upright he slapped my face so hard I reeled backward falling face first onto the bed. He immediately jumped onto my back straddling me and with his lips as close to my ear as possible, he hissed, "Don't ever think you can even begin to run my life, Violet. I will not let you or anyone tell me what to do."

He crawled off my back and flipped me over to where he could glare directly into my face.

"Do we understand each other?" he said his breath reeking of alcohol.

When I didn't answer he raised his arm back as if to strike me again, but for some reason thought better of it. He slid off the bed and ran into the doorframe on the way out of the room. He was muttering and cursing to himself as I heard the door to the hotel room slam shut.

I lay there too afraid to move or make a sound for what seemed like the longest time. I was so horrified by what had just taken place my emotions were frozen. The dimness in my room was only broken by the frenetic pattern of the tree limbs outside my window, lit from below by the flickering gas streetlamp.

I got up around 5 A.M. and went to the bathroom. I expected a bruised face when I turned on the light, but there was no evidence left of the abuse I had suffered. Only in memory and in my heart did the hot searing pain of the slap remain.

With shaking hands, I fixed myself a cup of hot tea and sat at the window and waited for the sun to rise. *God in Heaven...what am I going to do?* I thought. I realized at that moment his drinking problem was more than just a temporary situation. His attacks on my parents were completely unfounded. Everyone who knew my parents loved them. Yes, my father was opinionated. But he loved me enough to want to protect me, and whose father didn't? Roland had not convinced me my parents were the problem. He was the problem and I knew it. I was sure of it. But, what could I do about it?

I decided I needed to waste no time in moving back home. It was one thing to live with a man with a drinking problem, but an emotionally and physically abusive man was another situation altogether.

I was gathering my things when I heard a small knock on the door. My heart began to pound and fear rose up instantly. I was frozen in the position of being bent over the bed stuffing my things into my bag, and couldn't move. It was as if, by some evil magic spell, someone had nailed my feet to the floor. The slight tapping came again.

"Miss Violet, Honey, it's me," Lemon called through the door.

"Lemon?" I whispered.

"Miss Violet, you up yet?"

I slowly walked towards the door, every step a sheer effort of will. I opened the door and allowed Lemon to enter. I still couldn't say anything. Lemon walked into the room and then looked at me. "Honey, are you all right? You're white as a ghost. Miss Violet?"

I turned toward the bedroom still unable to say anything and walked straight toward the chair next to the bed. I slumped into it and lay my head back on the cushioned headrest.

Violet

Lemon glanced at my poorly begun attempt at packing and shook her head. Then taking off her hat and putting it with her bag on the bed, she started packing and repacking. When she had my things in order, she called down to the bellboy.

"Miss Violet, let's get your hair combed and put on your coat.

"If we call for a carriage, we can be at home in time for breakfast. Come on, now. Come sit in this chair in front of the vanity."

With Lemon coaching me, I soon had myself together just as the bellboy arrived.

I listened as Lemon called Coffeyville Wagon & Carriage Works, where she had taken the buggy to have the wheelwright mend a broken spoke.

"Mr. Herbert Buzard, please." There was a pause while she waited and she smiled at me.

"This is Lemon Jacobs, Mr. Buzard. Is the carriage ready? …oh that's wonderful. Thank you so much. Just send it down front of the Eldridge, please. Yes, my mamma is doing real well…"

"Thank you, Mr. Buzard."

She hung up the phone and said, "Come on, Baby girl, let's go home."

"What about Roland's things, Lemon?" I asked hesitantly.

"Don't you worry, Miss Violet. I'll send someone to fetch them, later."

I didn't look back as we left the hotel. Once again, Roland Murdock had shown his true self. I didn't know what I was going to do yet. I would have to think long and hard about everything before discussing the events of the night before with my parents. If I went to Papa with all that happened since my wedding day, he would have a posse rounded up within the hour. It wasn't that I wanted to protect Roland. The hard sting of that slap still rang through my memory and the vile vicious words that accompanied it. No, it wasn't Roland I was protecting. I had a child to think about, and my own reputation. God help me, I would think long and hard before I made any decisions about what to do about Roland Murdock.

Chapter XVI

October finally arrived. That fall, we had an Indian summer that lasted right up to the end of September. Oh, it was lovely, the only thing about my life at that point, that was.

My morning sickness was over, but my general health was poor. I'm sure it had everything to do with my mental health, which most days bordered on major depression.

Roland continued his drunken outrages. He would remove me from the house, conveniently under the guise of a carriage ride, only to berate and verbally abuse me after we would get a few blocks away. He knew he couldn't get away with this under the watchful eyes of my family.

His wasn't happy with his work. He wasn't happy with me. My pregnancy was rarely mentioned, except for when he was berating me for ruining his life. I had learned that Roland always found someone else to blame for whatever was his most current misery.

My physician, Dr. Starry, had informed me on my previous office visit that it was imperative that I begin to eat better and get more sleep. He thought the dark circles under my eyes were due to lack of rest. How was he to know it was from a complete lack of emotional support from my husband? I was too humiliated to tell him. Dr. Starry had been our family doctor for years and I couldn't bear his knowing the shame of what I was living day to day. I think he probably knew, as I wasn't much of an actress. A woman, who has just recently married, and expecting her first child, usually doesn't have the pallor of a prison inmate, kept in solitary confinement.

There were days that I would resolve to be happy, no matter what, if only for the sake of the child I was carrying, only to end up an emotional wreck after another carriage ride. Momma finally caught on to what Roland was doing, and the daily rides for "my air" began taking place with her while Roland was at the paper.

Construction continued in full swing on the mansion and with its length of over a hundred feet and width of forty-five feet, plus verandas, it was a commanding structure indeed. It was starting to look like a real southern mansion, but it was still not quite ready to move into. There had been some labor problems during the years the house was being built. There was the time that some of the men on the construction crew decided to strike, demanding more wages, and Papa found the leader of the strike, knocked him cold with one punch of his huge hand, and locked him in a boxcar which was headed out of town. The other workers decided maybe their pay wasn't so bad after all and went back to work.

Papa wasn't feeling well that particular fall. His stomach was giving him trouble again. Momma had Lemon preparing special foods like cream soups and custards, as he was more comfortable when eating bland foods. He wasn't happy about it though. He enjoyed his fried chicken and meat with rich sauces. Momma did her best to keep things calm and quiet and had informed the employees of their various businesses that they were to contact her, not Papa, with any problems or concerns. When you were sick, my Momma made it her number one concern to bring you back to good health. It was always a little frightening though when Papa would have these bouts with his stomach, as I had never forgotten the time Momma and I had found him unconscious by the side of the road after we went looking for him when he didn't show up for supper one hot summer night.

It was around the summer of 1901. Supper came and went and Papa hadn't gotten home from checking on some fences around the perimeter of our farm. Momma and I went to look for him in her little Phaeton carriage and found him at the far southeast corner of the farm, practically hidden in the tall grass. If not for his horse standing idly by his side, we might never have seen him in the tall summer grass. He was in a semi-conscious state and could do nothing to help us as we tried to load him into the carriage. My Papa was a huge man, and Momma and I quite weak in comparison, but we managed miraculously to get him home. When we were close enough to the greenhouse that had been built for Momma, she began to yell for help. By the time we reached the kitchen door there were plenty of strong farm hands to help carry him into the house. Lemon ran to call Dr. Starry as we rushed through the door and everything on the kitchen table was brushed to the floor in one fell swoop as the men gently lowered him onto it. We could see no obvious signs of blood, bumps, bruises, or broken bones. The only sign of anything wrong was the pallor of his summer-tanned skin and the clamminess when we would pat his cheeks for a response or grasp his hand. Momma and I stood back horrified as the men assessed Papa one after the other; discussing among themselves what could be the matter.

Dr. Starry finally arrived and the men surrounding Papa moved out of the way so he could be examined. He quickly took control of the room and ascertained that Papa appeared to be low on blood, and could possibly be bleeding internally. An ulcer was the suspected culprit, Dr. Starry had said, as he knew Papa quite well and knew how stressful all his business ventures were. He figured the fall from the horse was probably due to the low blood count not allowing enough oxygen to flow into the brain.

In the early morning hours, Papa finally became coherent enough to ask what had happened to him, and Momma and I explained. Once he realized he wasn't dying, his manner improved and he informed Momma and me that we were silly to have stayed up all night and worried about him. Dr. Starry instructed Momma that Papa was going to have to make some changes in his life; quit becoming so easily frustrated and volatile over small issues, and to calm down and take life a little easier. We weren't at all sure he was capable of making those changes. With color beginning to return to his face and with Dr. Starry assuring us that with rest, and the proper food, Papa would feel much better. We had worried about him ever since. He'd always been so strong and such a physical presence, it was hard to believe anything could happen to him. Momma and I had been extra considerate of him since then, whether he liked us fussing over him or not.

It was almost Halloween. The trees had turned brilliant orange and gold all over the grounds and I spent a lot of my time outside walking down to the river and sitting on the porch swing reading. I loved to read. Mystery novels had been my favorite. In fact, I used to love the suspense and the feeling of being slightly afraid. However, since marrying Roland, I found myself to be afraid more often than not and had changed my preferred reading to something more pleasant and uplifting. Donald loved to be read to, so we would sit on the swing and I would read aloud his favorite adventure stories that all little boys enjoy.

The day before Halloween dawned clear and bright with that first north breeze that suggests winter isn't far. I had walked down to the river after breakfast to sit on the bank and contemplate my life. The river had a way of soothing my most anxious thoughts. I was on my way back and had reached the last small rise to the east of the mansion when I was seized with a cramping sensation so intense it doubled me over. The pain seemed to go on forever. When it began to recede, I struggled to straighten up and get home. I had gotten only a few steps when the band of steel contracted against my abdomen again.

Oh, my God, oh, my God, I've got to get to the house, I thought, completely panic-stricken. As soon as the pain lessened I walked as fast as I could to make it to the bend where the mansion was in view. Maybe one of the construction crew would notice me. I wasn't the naive girl I had been just a few months earlier; I knew exactly what was happening. I was going to lose my baby if I didn't get help. With the next cramp I fell to the ground and I lay there doubled over in the fetal position with perspiration breaking out across my brow in spite of the cool breeze.

"I've got to get up and keep moving," I said out loud. "Oh, God. Please, someone help me." I called in vain as I was still too far away for anyone to hear me. Lemon would still be in the kitchen cleaning up, Momma would probably be in the greenhouse, which was her morning habit, and Papa was always checking on the crew and going over their plans for the day after breakfast. He could be anywhere on the property.

There was no one.

The cramping became so severe there was no more attempting to go anywhere. My body was completely engulfed in agonizing pain. All I could do was lie there and endure the cramping, wave after wave. The perspiration ran down my face and I was becoming too weak to even call out. I could feel the sun on my face and I knew that time was passing. I could only lie there and pray.

Someone will come looking for me, I thought. *Did anyone know I was even going down to the river?* Thoughts circled my brain, round and round.

The pain was becoming more severe and now the cramping was accompanied by a steady flow of what I knew could only be blood.

"Oh, God, please let someone come and find me before it's too late," I begged.

No one came.

The sun was directly over the trees by the time I started hearing voices calling.

It was Momma who found me.

She came around the bend in the trees calling my name and when she saw me, she began to run.

"Violet, Violet, Honey...what's happened?" She was screaming as she raced towards me. "Violet...................!"

She collapsed next to me in the grass and grabbed my hand. "What's happened, what's happened," she begged.

"The baby," was all I managed to get out before another spasm racked my body. I rolled up tight again and fought against the urge to scream out loud.

Momma began to hurl Papa's name out across the distance that separated them. "Papa...Papaaaaaaa....Will...!" she wailed.

He came tearing around the corner of the clearing, face white, out of breath. "Nannie K., what is...My God, what's happened to Violet?" He fell down in the grass beside Momma and I, and tried to get me to uncurl from my balled up position.

I couldn't do it. I was frozen in pain and terrified of what was happening. He finally reached underneath me and began to lift me into his arms. As his hands came around the other side of my body and he began to lift me up, Momma gasped.

Papa's hands were blood red.

"Oh, my God, Will, she's lost the baby...she's lost the baby," Momma sobbed.

Roland was, if nothing else, a very convincing actor. He was sympathetic, kind, and most attentive. Papa called him home from the paper and he was there within moments.

They had taken me upstairs to my room and Momma and Lemon had cleaned me up, dressed me in a nightgown and tucked me gently into my bed. Throughout the entire process, I had said not a word to either of them; just let the tears quietly fall down my cheeks with no attempt to wipe them away. They softly murmured to me, the way women will do in times of tragedy, and went about the task of making me as comfortable as they could. The cramping had stopped completely. It was done. The baby was gone.

Roland sat in the chair next to the bed after Momma and Lemon had gone and reached out for my hand.

"Everything will be all right, Violet. Don't worry," he said in his most rehearsed actor voice.

"You can leave me now, Roland," I said, as I turned toward the wall away from him.

"I will in a moment. I just want to make sure you can rest."

"That's not what I meant," I replied.

"What are you talking about?" he asked, confused.

"I mean you can leave now. There's no reason for you to stay any longer. You have no obligation to me...you're free," I said, staring at the wall.

"Violet, you just rest and quit talking nonsense. I'll be back later to check on you," he replied softly.

He quietly left the room. *"It's over now,"* I thought. A quiet calm settled over me. Instead of the tears and anguish I had expected when the door closed, there was only peace. It was as if the Lord, Himself, had covered me with a mantle of warmth and tranquility. I was so tired I couldn't stare at the wall another minute. I closed my eyes and drifted into a sleep that would last for almost two days.

The Christmas season came and with it the decision that we would move to Wichita and make a fresh beginning. For these last six weeks, Roland had been supportive and loving, with no drunken episodes or angry outbursts. I had assured him he could go without me, but he wouldn't hear of it. The job at the paper in Coffeyville was "unfulfilling" he had informed me, and he wanted to get back to work at *The Wichita Eagle*. We would live with his parents until we made other arrangements and would leave after Christmas.

As much as I fought against it, I began to feel hopeful once again about our marriage. Maybe there was a chance for it. I had talked to Momma about how I felt and she had encouraged me to continue on with the marriage as I had made vows and had an obligation to God and my husband. She had assured me we were over the worst hurdle and things would get better and better. I wanted so much to believe her.

The day after Christmas we left. I would start my new life in Wichita, Kansas. *Please let this be the answer,* I silently prayed.

Chapter XVII

We moved in with Roland's parents at 1616 Park Place in Wichita in January1905. The Murdock home was on a tree-lined street in one of the most beautiful neighborhoods in Wichita. It was spacious and beautiful. The two-story home had large white columns across the front, and shutters on every window that were painted the palest of yellows. It gave the house a warm comforting appearance. Roland reached for the doorknob of the front door, pushed it open and allowed me to enter before him. There stood his mother in the entryway. She welcomed me politely, but was as aloof as I had grown accustomed to her being over the past six months.

I decided from the time I realized we were moving to Wichita that I would give it my best, and try to move on with my life. I would get used to his mother's opinion of me and try not to let it interfere with my future. Maybe, in time, she would change her mind about me. I wasn't used to people not liking me as I had always been so accepted and well thought of at home in Coffeyville and at boarding school. This woman was my first challenge at learning you can't control how other people feel about you. I didn't like it, but was willing to let it alone and see if she would come around. I had discussed the situation with Momma when trying to make my decision to come to Wichita or not, and she had assured me that Louise Murdock would never treat me with disrespect or rudeness, and eventually she would be won over by my personality and wit. So far it hadn't happened.

Roland had given up on the paper in Coffeyville, and wanted to be back at *The Wichita Eagle*. He wasn't cut out for management, but wouldn't admit it.

Life in Wichita was faster paced than I was used to, but I found myself quickly fitting in. There were plenty of parties to attend and there was always a theater group in town performing. We went out a lot as Roland had plenty of friends and their wives and girlfriends readily accepted me.

By the time we were in Wichita a month, I began to feel a change in Louise Murdock. She had been so hesitant to accept me as her daughter-in-law, but as the days passed and we shared almost every meal together, her attitude toward me had begun to change. The first thing I noticed was that she had started making more eye contact with me when we had "meal" conversation. But, the biggest change, and the most significant, was the evening I came upon her, quite by accident, crying in the rose garden in the Murdock backyard.

I had been reading after supper and found myself starting to dose off, and it was much too early for bed. Putting on my sweater, I went out the terrace door for a breath of air. It was a mild February night and I felt immediately invigorated by the crispness of the moonlit evening. I had stepped off the terrace and started down the rose garden path, not having gone far when I heard the sound of muffled crying. Rounding the corner of the path, I found her sitting on a cold marble bench, weeping into her hands.

I sat down next to her and placed my hand on her shoulder not saying a word. When she spoke, it was in a voice wrenched with regret.

"Violet, I'm so very sorry," she sobbed, taking hold of my hands and pulling them toward her heart.

"Whatever for, Mrs. Murdock?" I answered quietly.

"I don't even know where to begin," she answered. "I've treated you abhorrently and I've blamed you for things I know now were not your fault. You are a fine and decent woman, and my son doesn't deserve you. I've had to protect him for most of his life from one mess after another. He's spoiled and arrogant, but I love him. He's my child – my only child, now. His father and I have given him everything, made things too easy for him, and I'm afraid we ruined him in the process. When you came into his life, I viewed you and the situation that had occurred as just another "incident" that needed to be solved. Getting to know you this past month has shown me how very wrong I was to have judged you prematurely. You have done nothing but treat me with respect when time after time I gave you every reason not to. I've come to know a young woman who shows much strength when times are hard, and I just want to ask you to forgive me for being so unfair." Her eyes had a desperate shining quality that had brought tears to my own eyes.

"Mrs. Murdock, of course I would forgive you, if there were anything to forgive. It's not been an easy time for any of us, and I'm just glad you've changed your mind about me. I was beginning to think everything I'd learned in charm school wasn't applying to me." I smiled and squeezed her hands. She tossed her head back and laughed softly in the moonlight.

"Oh, you dear girl. How in the world did my son find such a jewel as you?"

We rose together up off the cold bench in the garden and moved into the house, where in the warmth of the kitchen we shared a cup of tea and finally began to have the relationship that I had always wanted us to have.

I made my first real friend the next day at the library. Her name was Bess Innes Galland. I was in the mystery aisle and totally immersed in looking for a good book, when we literally bumped into each other. As we both turned to look, recognition dawned.

We had been to the same parties over the past month and our husbands knew each other well. We went to a nearby table and sat down to talk about our love of books, and life in Wichita. That was the beginning of a wonderful friendship; in fact, we were inseparable from then on. We would go on carriage rides together in my Phaeton, and she would marvel at how well I handled a carriage and horse, while teasingly informing me that "ladies" in Wichita didn't drive their own carriages.

As our friendship grew stronger we began to share more intimate details of our lives together, and I found her marriage to be as unfulfilling as mine. As hard as I was trying, Roland and I had a very strained relationship. There wasn't the closeness and intimacy I saw in my own parents, the spontaneous hugs and kisses. He was definitely much happier now that we were in Wichita, but that was due to being back in familiar surroundings and having his old friends back in his life.

Having found a friend of my own was a godsend and made the days in Wichita easier to bear. I missed my family terribly and wanted nothing more than to return home, but after meeting Bess,

I found myself enjoying Wichita. Living there became more of an adventure than an exile.

In May of that year, Donald developed a severe case of measles. He was five years old and by that time, Papa and Momma had hired a French governess, Mrs. Hughson, to watch over Donald.

Donald and Mrs. Hughson had been having their breakfast in the dining room when she noticed his eyes were swollen and red, and he seemed to be having difficulty breathing. He had no appetite whatsoever.

He ran a high fever and was terribly ill for the next four days. There were eruptions in his mouth; his skin was blotchy and dusky. He had a rash on his face and back, chills and vomiting. Dr. Starry had Momma keep him in a warm, airy room with muted sunlight and had her protect his eyes with screens so his eyelids would not form adhesions. By the fifth day, he began to improve, but his skin still showed a brownish stain where the eruptions had been.

Momma called me daily to give me reports on him, and by the third day of his illness I made the decision that I needed to go home.

The sight of his pale skin and lifeless little body terrified me. He looked so small and frail in the half-darkened room. When he saw me, he brightened somewhat, but he was so weak he could barely lift his hand to acknowledge me. For the next three days we all continued to nurse him around the clock until we felt the worse was over.

It wasn't until Momma and I were sitting in the kitchen one night very late that we both realized how frightened we all were. Talking quietly, making comparisons on how well we thought he was doing, Momma's voice began to shake, and her hands began to tremble.

"We can't lose him, Violet," she said, so softly I had trouble understanding her.

"Momma, of course we're not going to lose him," I replied, as I reached for her hand. "Nothing's going to happen to Donald."

"I couldn't stand it, Violet. I don't think I could live through it, again," her voice was so weak and strained with the effort to not spill tears.

"Oh, Momma, please don't cry…please don't worry. Donald's going to be just fine. Dr. Starry said so." I was trying so hard to convince her. And convince myself.

"Violet, do you remember how awful it was when we lost Willie?" She sobbed, the tears now flowing freely. "How sudden it all was? Tell me that isn't going to happen again. Tell me God isn't going to take my last son."

Papa walked into the kitchen at that moment, saw the look on both our faces, the tears streaming, and gathered us both into his arms, rocking us back and forth until the tears abated.

"No creator of the world could be that cruel," he said, in a voice filled with all the confidence he could muster. The silence in that room was deafening. Not one of us could be sure of anything, and hard as he tried to be convincing, we all three knew how unfeeling the hand of fate could be.

Chapter XVIII

In the heat of the summer that same year, we finally got to move into the "mansion" as Papa often called it. It wasn't completely finished, and wouldn't be for years to come, but enough so that Papa couldn't stand it any longer and decided it was time. I was grown and married, but the excitement of moving in consumed us all. I came home and helped with the unpacking. Roland was too busy with his friends and his night life, so he chose not to accompany me.

Donald was on the mend and excited about his new room. He hadn't regained his usual spunk, but Dr. Starry assured us that in time he would. Measles was a very serious illness in those days and it took some time to recover fully from it. Momma had pampered and spoiled him to the point where finally Papa told her she would make a sissy of him if she didn't turn him over to his care. So, Donald was finally back to checking fences on horseback with Papa and running errands with him into town and being his little companion. He loved helping out in the stables, brushing and grooming the horses. He was so interested in every detail that went on at the farm, and especially farm machinery itself. He would spend hours sitting on the veranda sketching out intricate details of how small engines were put together. This, of course, made Papa quite proud as he was sure it was a sign of great intelligence. Donald was most definitely a unique and talented child. As his older sister, I couldn't have been prouder of him and always looked forward to the time spent at home with him.

The house had turned out to be more magnificent than I had ever dreamed it would. It was massive, but without the cold austerity that most mansions can have. It was light-filled at all times of the day, the windows being made large enough to allow in as much light as possible. Papa had almost lost a business to fire some ten years earlier, so he had one of the first private homes with a fire hose built into the wall to avoid the devastation that a fire could cause. And there were so many closets! Closets for cleaning supplies, closets for linens, medicines, fabric storage, and closets just standing empty waiting for a purpose to be thought up. The bedrooms had closets in an age when size increased property taxes, but Papa didn't care. "I can afford it!" He would say gleefully, his eyes just gleaming. . . He was so proud of our new home.

Momma had been purchasing furniture for the house in the past six months and she had artfully blended new pieces with old and added accessories to go with each and every room. In the front parlor, which faced the south and west, she used light colored small settees that suited her size and were comfortable for her. She informed Papa this room would be where she would entertain her guests as it was suited to a ladies parlor. Across the hall was the main living area and this was where she placed all of his most favorite pieces of furniture. This room included the wonderful Inglenook and Momma had overstuffed cushions made for it and it looked quite cozy tucked into the wall, just like a private hiding place where I could disappear with a book on a rainy afternoon.

The main entry to the house was impressive with the front door being designed by Mr. Tiffany and the leaded glass windows made in his workshop. It faced the west and the sunsets were divine. Papa even had a billiard room with its own fireplace. There were eight fireplaces in the house! But, I was most excited about my bedroom which was at the west end of the upstairs and was decorated with a pale green paint with a hand-painted violet pattern that went all around the room up near the ceiling. Momma had a wool rug made from the wool of our very own sheep that included a violet pattern as well. Oh! it was lovely. The third floor, which would be finished last, would be a ballroom that had terraces outside where the band members could set up their instruments and not interrupt the flow of the room.

Momma had been working on the landscaping of the yard for years already and her pride and joy was her greenhouse. There were fruit trees, flowers and even vegetables growing in there all year round. She loved working in that greenhouse. She said working with the soil of the earth was like therapy to her and she was never happier than when she was mixing potting soil and growing something new and exotic. After the small plants that she had babied became big enough to be houseplants, she would carefully put them in beautiful pottery planters and bring them into the solarium which was always alive with plants of every size and shape. Momma loved to grow things and she was good at it.

It was a joy to all of us to be finally able to move into the elegant mansion that my father and mother had planned and nurtured through its every stage. Our first night there, Momma sat at the grand piano in the music room and played for us; something she had promised Papa she would do as soon as we moved in. She promised there would be lots of music coming from this room in the years to come. She loved to play and it had been years since she had been able to.

W.P. Brown, my Papa, had finally been able to give his family the home of his dreams. He couldn't have been more proud to see how happy it made all of us. He had worked so hard for this house and all it stood for. He was the hardest working man I had ever known and I couldn't have been more proud of what he had accomplished.

Chapter XIX

Papa discovered a radium well on our land in the early fall of 1905. Experts were called in from all over the country and drilling began. Down through the Mississippi limestone they drilled under which was Silurian sandstone, and after drilling hundreds of feet further through the hardest of rock they finally burst through to one of the finest mineral water springs ever discovered. This flow of mineral water when first drawn out was a greenish-yellow color and smelled of sulfur from the hydrogen sulfide, a gas that burns with a pale blue flame and gives out the odor of sulfur. Before this gas is burned it smells like decaying eggs. This was the gas that was present in the water of Sulfur Springs, Virginia, and in other famous spring waters. It was judged to be valuable medicinal sulfur mineral water by the chemist's after smelling and tasting it and was reported to be the best of curative and healthful waters.

The use of mineral water for medicinal purposes began before the beginning of recorded history. The Greeks and Romans used mineral water for remedial purposes from their earliest days. About 400 B.C. the Greek physician, Hippocrates, wrote a book in which he discussed this very thing. The Romans had long before discovered thermal springs in Italy. Other nations and cultures did likewise. Invalids have used the sulfurous thermal springs since biblical times as a treatment for illness of all kinds. Some of these waters achieved worldwide fame, such as Vichy and Seltzer.

Native Americans used the springs in America, and the Mohawks brought Sir William Johnson, the British superintendent general of Indian affairs, to bathe in their springs in 1776. In the late 19th century, the spots for taking the mineral water became fashionable with elaborate facilities for the patrons.

Papa was excited and ready for a new enterprise as most of the mansion was finished and things were starting to slow down there. He drew up plans for a bathhouse and natatorium that would bring in people from all over the United States and Europe. The building was to be constructed of brick and would be two stories high. An architect was hired to begin the planning of a park and lake with a concrete bottom. This was to be one of the greatest health resorts in the world!

Papa boasted to Momma that his spa would become the World's Best Turkish and Mineral Water Bathhouse, containing a gymnasium, barbershop, and clubrooms. There would be golf, tennis, basketball and other sports facilities, including a swimming pool. In the facility, he explained to us, there would be hairdressers, manicurists, and masseuses who would cater to the wealthy clientele from all over the globe. Papa even wanted a medical doctor on staff at all times for the treatment of the guests as some would be recuperating from illnesses and would need special care. He hired Dr. W.T. Shipp to be the medical director and supervise all aspects of building the Natatorium. Dr. Shipp put together a staff of ten consulting physicians as well.

Papa, always wanting to be as impressive as possible, decided the swimming pool would be the biggest in the West, twenty feet wide, one hundred feet long and ten feet deep. The water in the indoor pool would be kept at an even seventy degrees.

The construction was soon underway. The huge structure began to take shape. No doubt about it, it was awe-inspiring. A veranda surrounded the entire building on two floors, so the patrons could sit outside and relax and enjoy the view of the countryside from all angles. The men and women's bath departments were 7,500 square feet. A most complete and elaborate ventilation system brought fresh air in and took stale air out. As the Silurian water required no filtering since its source was subterranean, it was always clear and sparkling, perfect for bathing.

Everything was planned and no detail overlooked. There were the medicinal baths, slabs for rubdowns, needle shower baths with individually controlled water temperature, hot and vapor rooms and two electric light bath cabinets of the newest design. The gymnasium was thirty-three feet by one hundred feet with both light and heavy fixtures for exercise.

Violet

As the construction progressed, Papa interviewed local people for various jobs. Good service would be key to the success in Papa's eyes. He wanted people who would be polite, well trained, and skilled. He made an excellent choice when he decided to hire Charley Robinson. Charley was a lightweight boxer who started his career at Churchill Downs in Kentucky. He had retired after 226 fights, and had become a trainer. Charley, and his wife, who was a pharmacist, were hired to manage the bathhouse. Charley's wife mixed all the liniments that were used for the rubdowns Charley would give the boxers after a training session. Charley was a trainer for our local boxers, and enjoyed preparing the men for their fights at the Memorial Hall.

Papa consulted with well-known physicians about the remarkable healing power of what was referred to as "the black water." This remarkable water was said to correct indigestion, constipation and diseases "peculiar to women." Intoxication could be cured without ill affects. The black water was thought to cure all disorders of the liver and stomach, purify the blood, remove all aches and pains and restore the exhausted individual back to rested health. Swimming was easy in this water because of the buoyancy from the mineral content.

The land surrounding the Natatorium was turned into a forty acre park filled with flowers, a lagoon with row boats and steam launches, and an open air swimming pool that was one hundred and fifty feet by three hundred feet and filled with sea water that ranged in depth from a few inches to fifteen feet.

In the park there were swings, slides, toboggans, and even a scenic railway ride.

It was spectacular when finished! Papa threw a grand opening party and invited everyone to come visit the newest attraction in Coffeyville. He brought in an orchestra to play. The floor of the gymnasium was thought to be the best in the country and a dance was held there. He gave away souvenirs and carnations for everyone who came through the door. Everyone in Coffeyville and the surrounding towns came out for this much-anticipated event. Papa was honored by all who attended and Mayor Wilcox of Coffeyville told the crowd, "I knew that it would be a success and that neither money nor energy would be spared to make it what it ought to be. I do not believe there is a man in Coffeyville who has done any more for this city than Mr.

Brown has." This statement brought applause from all parts of the building.

Papa was in his glory. The first year the spa was opened, people came from all over the United States, England and France. It was not unusual at all to take in $5000.00 per day. It became one of the most popular and pleasant places to be. Everyone enjoyed it, from the very young to the very old and infirm. Donald especially loved to go to the Natatorium with Grant, Lemon's son. Grant and Donald were the same age and had developed a close friendship growing up together. They would have a swim, or work out on the rings in the gymnasium. They loved spending time with Charley, too. Everyone who knew Charley felt that way.

After the death of his wife, we invited Charley to move into the mansion with us. We gave Charley the butler's quarters in the basement. He was of great help to all of us and enjoyed staying busy. Momma would invent little projects to keep him active, as he was quite elderly by then. Charley died on a cold winter day in 1955. He had become quite a fixture around the Natatorium, or the "Nat" as it was referred to, and at the mansion as well. He had many friends, was an inspiration to all who knew him and his smiling face and cheerful disposition could always be counted on to cheer you on an otherwise dreary day.

Once again, W.P. Brown, that entrepreneur of the turn of the century, was famous. Even Papa himself would marvel at the accomplishments he had made over the course of his forty-four years.

Chapter XX

In January of 1906, I lost a second child. This one I carried almost to term. It was a tiny baby boy. He lived for five days. Roland continued to abuse me, both physically and emotionally. These kinds of subjects were not discussed. In those days, you kept your marital business within your own four walls and suffered in silence. You either put up with it, or one day you just disappeared and never came back. I wanted to choose the latter, but it would take me a few more years to find the courage. My marriage was in name only.

By 1908, I was spending my time between Wichita and Coffeyville, going home more and more frequently to be with my family and, of course, my dear friend, Sophie. She looked so forward to my visits as her situation at home was tenuous as ever in regard to her father and his attitude toward his daughters having any kind of life outside the walls of his home.

Donald had long since recovered from his bout with the measles, but was never quite as healthy again. He was pale and drawn, his energy level only half of what it had been. He had undergone more than one tooth extraction due to abscesses and ulcerations. Momma and Papa tried vigilantly to keep him fit and happy, but he was a mere shadow of the boy he had been before. My parents installed rings in the ceiling of the ballroom and hired a personal trainer to come in and work with Donald to build up his strength.

One summer evening when I was home, Momma and I were sitting on the veranda looking out at the setting sun, and I decided to tell her just how bad things were between Roland and me. The only people I had talked to about this had been Bess and Sophie, and I longed for the sympathy and understanding I could only receive from my mother. She knew my marriage was not as it should be. There was no way to keep that from a family as close as ours. As we sat and talked, swinging back and forth on the porch swing, the conversation turned to a young family in town who were having a rocky time in their marriage, and I decided I had the perfect opportunity to get a few things off my chest.

"Momma, has your marriage to Papa always been a happy one?" I asked, hesitantly.

"Where in the world did that come from, Violet?" she asked, surprised.

"Well, it's just something I've often wondered about. By the time I was old enough to think about things like that, you had been married for years, and I'm just curious, I guess."

"Well, I won't deny that your father and I had a few rough spots in the road. You know your father. He likes things to be his way, and I had to spend a few years there in the beginning learning to accept that. But, I loved him so much, most of the time I didn't mind giving more than he gave. He was so busy in those early years trying to make a living and he worked such long hours. He didn't always have a lot of time for me, but it was because he was working so hard to make a life for us. Your father and I have worked very hard to make a good life with each other. I can honestly say that I feel like my marriage to your father has been a good one. We love each other very much. Why are you asking about this now, Violet?"

"All young girls dream of how their married lives will be, Momma. I always thought I'd fall in love, have a fairytale marriage, and live happily ever after just like in the storybooks. My marriage to Roland has been anything but that. You know he doesn't treat me like Papa treats you. As much as I've tried, Momma, he has never let me into his heart. I'm not sure he even has a heart."

"Oh, Violet, come now. Life is not a storybook and marriage is not a fairytale. You two have weathered the storms of early marriage and things should be fine by now."

"But they're not, Momma. The truth is, I'm in a loveless marriage. I'm married to a man who couldn't care less about me. He never holds me, or kisses me, never even looks at me when I'm in the same room with him."

"Violet, he's your husband, of course he loves you."

"Momma, how can you say that? You know how he is. You've seen him when he's drunk. How can you defend him? My marriage is horrid and you know it," I implored.

"All I know is that you took vows to love, honor and obey your husband, and as the young woman that your father and I brought you up to be, that's exactly what you need to continue doing. Why don't you think about having another baby?"

"What?...Momma haven't you heard a single word I've said to you? A baby is the last thing this rotten marriage needs. Why would I want to bring an innocent little baby onto this sinking ship? For heaven's sake, Momma."

That was the end of that conversation. I excused myself from the swing and went into the house. I paced back and forth in frustration. I looked outside a few moments later and watched Momma as she continued to swing back and forth totally unfazed by our conversation. Her thoughts were, I'm sure, on Donald and his poor health. *I can't live like this much longer,* I thought. *With or without my parents' blessing, I just can't.*

By 1909, Donald's health was worsening again. He had one cold after another. He was easily fatigued. We were all worried sick about him. In mid-December, after months of tests, he was diagnosed with Type I diabetes. Dr. Starry informed us that all the symptoms were present and he was as sure as it was possible to be that the diagnosis was correct. Donald had lost his appetite completely, was nauseated, tired and restless, he was dizzy, and had ringing in his ears. There were even disturbances in his breathing.

Momma immediately began her quest to make him well. Lemon and Momma researched everything known on diabetes at the time. There were oatmeal treatments, milk treatments, wheat flour, and potato treatments. Nothing seemed to be helping. Donald was becoming weaker and weaker. His body was simply not producing the insulin it needed. Without insulin, the glucose cannot enter the cells of the body to provide energy. The cells are forced to burn fat to get the energy they need, and the body begins to literally starve itself to death.

Donald was given a high calorie diet and as much liquid as he could tolerate to combat the dehydration. He slowly lost weight anyway.

Weeks passed into months. I spent more and more time in Coffeyville with my family. I rarely went to Wichita at all. Roland would come down to Coffeyville every other weekend or so, and that soon became less. I felt nothing but relief when he would call and leave messages with Lemon that he wasn't coming. I didn't care anymore.

Sophie came to the house almost daily. Her love and concern were heartfelt. I don't know what I would have done without her. She would take walks with me to the river, and we would occasionally go to the Opera House and take in a show.

Momma and Papa were losing heart, as Donald became weaker and quieter. It wouldn't be long before he would be bedfast. The doctors were doing everything they could to help him, but there was so little they could do. Almost everything was known about insulin deficiency at this time; that this deficiency caused the disease, but until the Toronto, Canada, group of Banting and Best discovered the way to supply the missing substance in 1922, diabetes was a killer. We were still years away from finding a cure for this illness.

Donald kept busy with the books he loved, and always had a sketchpad nearby when he wanted to draw. He was virtually bedfast by 1910. The doctors were amazed that Momma had been able to keep him alive. Lemon would bake special treats for him and sing to him as she bathed him, anything to make him comfortable. Lemon's son, Grant, would sit by Donald's bedside and tell him what was going on in town with their friends, just spending time with him. They had been so close all their young lives.

I spent hours reading him books and telling him stories that I made up; stories full of adventure, intrigue and mystery. He would reward me with a wan little smile, breaking my heart with love for him.

How could such a precious little boy have become so terribly sick? I prayed like I had never prayed before that a miracle would happen and Donald would beat this dread disease, but you could see on a daily basis how it was taking over his body with no mercy, no conscience whatsoever.

Chapter XXI

After many long talks with Sophie and Bess, I decided to leave Roland and seek a divorce. Seven years of marriage, seven years of physical abuse, mental anguish and heartache. It was time to end it. Not wanting any fight from him and not wanting my private matters displayed in the courts in Kansas where a reporter might latch onto the dismal details, I took the train to California. With the help of my attorney, I had secured an apartment in San Diego, so I could establish residency there.

I learned of a treatment facility for diabetes in San Diego in the fall of 1910. Several of our family friends had made suggestions about treatments they had heard about, but we were always hearing of some new alternative medical treatment; most were worthless. This program sounded legitimate and I wanted to check it out. I visited the clinic run by Dr. Francis Mead, the chief medical officer for the city of San Diego. I was impressed and felt that it was a real chance to save my dear little brother, so I sent for Momma to bring Donald.

The clinic was just a few blocks from the apartment. We got Donald checked in and prayed fervently for him to get well. We were so full of trust and hope.

At the end of six weeks of treatment, we seemed to see a ray of hope in the doctor's eyes, and Donald was looking a little better. He even seemed to have a little more energy. He was more talkative than he'd been in months, and had asked to see the ocean again.

We planned a visit for the next week and he looked forward to it eagerly. We talked of the seashells we would find and the sandcastles we would build together.

The morning of the planned trip to the ocean, Momma and I arrived early at the clinic. Chattering happily, we made our way down the hall to his room, talking of the day we would all have together. Rounding the corner, we immediately saw a group of doctors standing outside Donald's door consulting each other with worried faces and talking in soft, quiet voices.

Momma reached out and gripped my hand and we proceeded past the doctors into Donald's room.

There he lay in the hospital bed, eyes sunken in their orbits, his lips dry and cracked. As I leaned over the bed to kiss him, his breath smelled unnaturally sweet. His breathing was rapid and heavy. He was so weak he could barely open his eyes.

Momma ran back out of the room.

"What's happened?" she cried to the doctors. "He was doing so much better."

"Mrs. Brown," Dr. Mead began. "It looks as if Donald has taken a turn for the worse. We've done everything humanly possible. It might be best to call your husband and have him come. Your son is in God's hands now."

He patted her softly on the shoulder and turned away to consult once more with the other doctors. They moved down the hall out of our range of hearing and we were left standing there not knowing what to do.

"Call your father..." she said softly. "He said to call your father, Violet. Oh, God, I know what that means..." She hung her head and cried quietly.

I was utterly speechless with grief. We were losing him.

After all the prayers, all the deals I had struck with God, the begging and pleading, He was going to take Donald from us, anyway. I walked back into his room and sat quietly by his bed, taking his small, frail hand into mine.

"Oh, Donald," I begged, "please try harder to get well. We can't go on without you. Don't you understand that? You must fight harder my precious little brother. You must fight! The world will stop for all of us if you leave. Please Donald, please, get well." The tears I cried were full of bitterness and anger.

How could fate be so cruel?

By the time Papa arrived, Donald had slipped into a coma. I watched my big strong father cry the tears of a child as he stood next to the bed, helpless and able to do nothing for the one he loved so

Violet

dearly. All we could do was keep watch over him until the angels came and took him to be with Willie.

The doctors had prepared us as best they could, so we knew it was only a matter of time. We had begged God and cried bitter tears. Now all we could do was hold his hand and whisper to him how much we loved him. And wait.

The beautiful child that we all had thought was to be ours forever was slipping away from us.

On October 12, 1911, at seven o'clock in the morning, Donald left us. Two hours later we boarded a train with his small body loaded onto one of the cars and started back home to Coffeyville. The trip would take many long days.

Momma was completely despondent. She uttered not one word. There was nothing we could do for her, nothing we could do for ourselves. The heartache was so intense we were numb.

We buried him next to his baby brother in the family plot in Elmwood Cemetery. My mother was never the same after that. All the life, all her spirit left with Donald. He had been, her greatest joy in life, her hope for the future. That was gone now. Donald's death changed all our lives forever. He was the most unique person I had ever known, and have never met anyone who could compare with him. He was talented, artistic, and incredibly intelligent. He was the light of our lives.

As I stood next to that tiny little grave that would hold my brother for all eternity, I remembered the morning I had gotten him out of bed and taken him to see the sun rise over the river. I had a sense then that it was something special and something I would forever remember…his beautiful little face lit from within with the excitement of something new.

Oh, how I've cherished that memory over the years, and oh, how I've missed him.

Chapter XXII

After Donald's death the family existed in a forlorn vacuum. The mansion was utterly silent, day in and day out. The servants even mourned. Everyone went about their daily chores in silence, merely going through the motions of living.

Sophie would come out daily and sit with me, holding my hand, trying her best to comfort me. One day, she told me she had met someone new. Her longtime boyfriend, John McCreary, had been gone to school for years by then and that relationship had fizzled out. Her father had finally given her permission to work part time at Wells Brothers clothing store in town. It pleased her so to be able to have something to look forward to each day and she enjoyed working in the store and selling items to the townspeople. One day a man came into the store and she offered to help him with his purchase. He was looking for a gift for his mother. Sophie suggested a pair of gloves. After she had finished with the sale, the young man thanked her and left. The next day, a note was waiting for Sophie when she arrived at work. It was from the young man, stating how much he had appreciated her help, and he was hoping to be allowed to see her again. She was excited by the prospect.

Later that day, this same man came into the store and asked her if she would go to Jordan-Florea's Drug Store for a chocolate soda when she finished working. A budding romance began. They met as often as possible at the drug store for sodas. Over the years, Sophie had had to make up many things outside the house for her father to think she was doing: social club meetings, church events, etc., because of his attitude on dating and men in general. Why she couldn't stand up to her father at her age was a mystery to me, but every time I tried to bring it up to her and discuss it, she would simply state the fact that there was no changing her father, and then dismiss the topic.

By the time they had been secretly meeting for a month, Sophie knew she was in love. She had been filling me in on every detail for weeks and you could tell from her expression that she had met the man she wanted to marry. She was in turmoil about the prospect of discussing it with her parents, but wanted to get it out in the open. Sophie was an honest person, and hated the feeling of deceiving her mother and father. She asked me in earnest one afternoon what she should do. I told her she needed to talk to her parents and remind them of the fact that she was a grown woman and entitled to a life of her own, even though all her grown sisters were still living at home and still under the rule of their father.

The next day she spoke with her parents and the outcome was as she had feared it would be. Her father was furious, accused her of being no better than a harlot, and forbade her to see the young man again. She was crushed. She came to the mansion in tears and after an hour of consoling her, she began to try to help me to understand her father.

"You don't understand, Violet, my father wants things to be a certain way," she tried to explain. "He expects all us girls to stay with him and Momma and keep the family together."

"That doesn't make any sense to me, Sophie," I reasoned. "You will always be family no matter if any of you marry or not. Why can't he see that?"

"There's no getting through to him," she cried.

"What about your mother? Why doesn't she try to help you?" I pressed.

"Momma's no help whatsoever. She does anything he says to do, and dares not go against him. She knows better," Sophie said with her head hung low, defeated.

"Go against him? What does that mean?"

"Oh Violet, you'll never understand what my life has been like, and I wish I could say more, but there's just no way to put it into words. I guess it's just hopeless." With that she did her best to dry her tears and then quickly decided she had to leave.

"Wait, Sophie, don't go yet. I know we can figure something out. I'll do anything I can to help you. You know I will. You've been such a wonderful friend to me. I want to help," I pleaded.

"There's really nothing you can do, Violet. I knew it would be like this. I knew my father would never let me go. He won't let any of us go…ever." Her eyes were fixed in a faraway stare and her voice was flat and emotionless.

She got up to leave. I rose from the chair to walk her out and when we got to the door, she turned and looked at me with eyes full of despair.

She took both my hands in hers and gazed deeply into my face. It was as if she were trying to memorize every feature one last time.

"I love you, Violet," she softly said. "You have been the best friend anyone could ever hope to have." She wrapped her arms around me and laid her head on my shoulder. "Goodbye," she said, still wrapped tightly in our embrace.

I pulled away from her and held her at arm's length trying to lighten the moment by smiling and fussing with her hair.

"You're a mess," I teased. "We'll get this all worked out, you'll see. You worry too much. This isn't the end of the world."

She touched my cheek with her tiny, soft fingertips and turned and walked out the door.

On Friday night of that same week Sophie stole away after work and went with a co-worker to the public dance held at Kloehr Hall. Shortly after midnight she arrived home. She went up to her room and dressed in her nightclothes.

She slipped the ring off her finger that she had received for her eighteenth birthday and placed it on the finger of her sleeping sister, Marguerite, who had chosen this night to sleep in Sophie's room. It was not unusual for Sophie to come home and find Marguerite asleep in her room, quite the contrary, would feel comforted by it.

She walked over to the bureau and took out the vial of carbolic acid she had attained some time before. Stepping to the bay window of her bedroom she opened one of the windows. In the moonlit recesses of the night, she raised the bottle of carbolic acid to her lips and drank the entire ounce that had been purchased. It was the only choice she felt she had left, the only way to be released from her father.

She stood in the light of the moonlit window and began to softly sing, mournfully. She lifted her voice to the heavens and sang one last song to the world.

Marguerite awoke at the sound of the whispered singing, and as she was sitting up in the bed, Sophie turned to look at her, turned back to the window, and then collapsed to the floor. Marguerite's screams woke the household.

Dr. Starry, who lived across the street, was called. Sophie was unconscious by the time he reached her and the doctor could see she was beyond any help. She languished until early morning and then passed on to the next world.

Her father told the authorities that his daughter had come in after midnight, but declared that he had "spoke gently" to her. The family commented that they had no idea what had caused this tragedy. They declared that Sophie was prone to "fits of despondency" and believed it was possible a "love affair might have been responsible."

The town was rocked once again with the trauma of another unexpected death. The vial of carbolic acid Sophie had taken bore the label of the Jordan-Florea Drug Store, but the druggist denied having sold it to Sophie or any member of the Gabler family.

How had she attained the poison? But no one knew. Even though, carbolic acid had become a way in which to take one's life had she really known what would happen? The drug, phenol, is a very corrosive, poisonous substance derived from coal tar. It was not a pleasant way to die. The body goes into convulsions, with rapid, deep breathing, and a drop in blood pressure. The lips and fingernails turn blue. The nervous system becomes hyperactive, and eventually the person slips into a coma. The face, lips and throat are burned in the process, but Sophie, remarkably, suffered no such adverse effects of the drug. Her beautiful face was unmarred by the corrosive liquid. The following Monday, I received an envelope in the mail. Inside was an entry from Sophie's diary. Printed in the upper left-hand corner in her small neat script was simply, "To my dear friend Violet...please forgive me."

December 14, 1911   My decision is made. There's no use in pretending anymore. I'm a prisoner and always will be. I don't even remember when this all started, just that it's been going on as long as I can remember...this nightmare that is called my family. Am

I the only one? Does he visit each of us in turn? How can he call himself a father? This can't be what father's do. He claims to love me. Love me? This isn't love. What kind of father comes into his daughter's room at night and lies down with her, forcing her to do the things he does. Why can't I remember when this started? Has it always been? I'm so confused I can't think straight anymore. I want out of this house and there's no escape. He told me I'm not fit to be with any man, that I'm ruined. Oh please, somebody, help me to understand this. Why do I call out for someone to help...there is no one...there's never been anyone. I feel as if Mother knows what he does to me. She sometimes looks at me with contempt in her eyes as if maybe I'm to blame. Am I to blame? Is that possible? I've decided to end my life; how, I don't yet know. Maybe a rope around my neck in the living room bay window. Wouldn't that say to the people in town, "Look, look, there's something very wrong in this house." I could use Father's gun...that would be appropriate to use his own weapon. How I hate him. Maybe I'll take him with me. Maybe I'll kill him slowly the same way he's been killing me slowly all my life. He's right about one thing...I'm ruined for any other man. One final note Dear Diary...my monthly hasn't come this month...God forgive me for what I have to do.

    I agonized over what I should do with this information for days before I made the decision. In the end I realized there was nothing I could do. Sophie and her sisters were victims of a mad man who walked around town portraying himself as a prominent citizen, loving father and husband. I finally came to the conclusion that I couldn't humiliate Sophie by telling anyone. It would forever be our secret. She had trusted me with the page from her diary and the secret would remain just that. I would let the townspeople think Sophie had been despondent over a love affair gone bad. That was better than the truth. The truth was too ugly to tell anyone, ever. Why didn't any of us figure it out? All the looks Momma and Papa would exchange at the mention of Sophie's name. The way Lemon would get so quiet when Sophie was around. Did they know? Or did they just know something wasn't quite right in that house?

    My beautiful childhood friend was dead at the age of twenty-two. Once again I had lost someone I held close to my heart. Sophie died in December, two short months after Donald's death.

Violet

The following week, Papa came to me and made a suggestion. He said he had given it a lot of thought and felt that a trip abroad might be good for me. He wanted to send me to Italy. At first the idea seemed absurd to leave at such a time, but the more I thought about it, the better the idea seemed to become. I had never wanted to get away from something more than I did Coffeyville at that moment. It was nothing but a constant reminder of how life seemed to be nothing but miserable endings of one kind or another.

I called my friend, Bess, in Wichita, and invited her to come along with me. She thought it was a marvelous idea. Papa would send me anywhere in the world with the hope that I could somehow recover from the losses that I had suffered the past few years.

Bess arrived a couple of days later and we boarded a train bound for California. From San Francisco we would leave for the Orient and then travel westward on another ship, to Europe stopping wherever we wished.

I would not return for at least a year.

Chapter XXIII

The villas along the coast were all cream colored and the sunlight made them glow with a warmth that attracted me. It would be wonderful to see them everyday for the rest of my life. The terra cotta tile roofs were a perfect compliment to the stucco walls. And the little towers on the top of the houses made me wonder if they were like the widow walks I had seen on the seacoasts of New England.

Sitting beneath a colorful umbrella, I played with the cold drink in my hand and relaxed in the comfortable chair. It wasn't the kind of beach I was used to. Here there wasn't endless sand so that I could take a walk and let the Atlantic Ocean pull at my feet. No dune grass grew here; no shells or starfish to pick up.

The Mediterranean, here at Livorno had stolen most of the sand, and would have taken all of it, along with the villas and the coastal highway. Here there were large piles of huge blocks of rock and cement, used to form breakwaters and artificial lagoons.

A day at the beach in Livorno meant changing into a swimsuit in a little cabana and sitting at a table with very good service, and if swimming was on the agenda, there was the lagoon. I did like the tall diving tower. It was similar to the one in the pool at the Natatorium. When I was younger and more carefree I had enjoyed using it.

When I arrived in Caen I would have a sandy beach on which to sun myself. But for the next two days, Bess and I would spend most of our time playing cards, when not enjoying the seaside life of Livorno.

Tonight there was a dinner party at the hotel. Bess Galland and I had been invited and I would go; even though I preferred going to bed early. But Bess had been adamant. She was sure that I needed to be pulled from depression and "frivolled up." I'm too serious for her liking. I've decided to be at least somewhat cooperative. Bess was a dear to come all the way to Europe with me.

Picking up my glass, I drank quite a bit of it. It tasted like punch, even had a reddish cast to it, but it was loaded with rum and it tasted wonderful. This "club," as the seaside establishments were called, used the best rum and dressed the drinks up with fruit and lots of ice.

Not for the first time, I wished that Lemon had come along. She had seen me through some of the worst days of my marriage, been a support to me. Lemon should be in Italy enjoying the sun, too. But Lemon had her family and Momma needed her more than ever, right now.

Donald's death had taken something out of my mother. I had always thought of her as vital, immortal. Now, I was afraid of losing her.

Papa will take care of her, I thought. They're devoted to each other. The two had always seemed to get through anything that fate threw at them. But losing their last son had almost taken them both down. From Momma's letters, Papa was spending almost all his time at work, and she sounded a little lonely.

A waiter stopped in front of me.

"Another drink, Signora?"

"Si." Watching him walk away, I admired his build and the way he moved. *I don't need any complications,* I thought and dismissed him from my mind and finished my drink.

Looking at my watch I saw that I would have to leave in the next half-hour if I wanted to make my hair appointment. The thought didn't appeal to me. Bess would be expecting me to be properly "frivolled," so I had to go.

Letting my eyes go to the deeply green and blue water, I lay back in the chair and watched the sparkling water trying to reduce the great blocks of rock to pieces. It wasn't like the Pacific with its lazy waves coming into the beach at San Diego, caressing the sand on the shore and retreating in a regular rhythm. Here the waves landed with determination and force, trying to create sand out of solid rock.

A fresh drink appeared in front of me and the empty glass was gone. I decided to only have a few sips and then head back to the hotel. Paying my bill, I entered the cabana and changed clothes.

There had been some slender, pretty women walking down the road a few evenings ago, in their abbreviated bathing suits, but I didn't have the figure or the confidence to try it. Putting on my street clothes, I regretted the heavy skirt. It was good for walking and a protection from stickers when I ventured off the road, but the day was hot and I wished for lighter fabric.

At the hotel, I took a quick shower, changed again, and returned to the lobby where I entered the beauty shop. Most of the beauticians didn't speak English, but I spoke Italian to the young woman and told her what I wanted, and sat down to wait. It was a short wait.

Returning to my room, I was in time to catch the phone still ringing.

"*Pronto.*"

"Violet?"

"Of course it's me, Bess. Are you calling to cancel?" I was still hoping that she could get out of the dinner party.

"No. I just wanted to make sure that you were back. I'll meet you in the lobby about five minutes before eight, okay?" Her tone was insistent, so I agreed to be there.

My new evening dress was from Paris and in two parts. The slip could be worn alone if one were daring enough and was of a peacock blue silk. The over tunic was of deep green lace and was very flattering to the arms. Bess was impressed and said so.

In the dining room a large table had been set up and decorated with low arrangements of some exotic looking flowers. *Momma would love those flowers!* I smiled to myself, and noticed I was a bit homesick. Our host and hostess greeted us and invited everyone to be seated. Thankfully, Bess and I were seated by each other. I wasn't up to producing any sparkling conversation tonight with some strange man, who probably spoke a language that I didn't know.

Seated across from me, was a very attractive Italian man. Ernesta, our hostess had introduced him as Antonio Bellini. He was tall and had light brown curly hair. With a smile, in a wonderful accent he often addressed himself to me. Though polite he made it plain that he was attracted.

In the ladies' room, Bess was very encouraging.

"Will you stop, Bess. I'm not ready to get involved with anyone, and I'm not interested in marriage."

"Actually that's an advantage, his wife might object if you were."

My mouth dropped open. "Are you serious? He's been flirting with me for over an hour and he's married?"

"Every good looking man in Italy is married, Violet. That doesn't keep them from having other relationships. Wives are very understanding around here." And Bess winked at me.

"And if their wives get involved with other men?" I ventured to ask.

"Not acceptable behavior for Italian wives. In the local paper the other day I read that a man killed his wife for fooling around and he got away with it!"

In bed that night, I lay awake for a time thinking about Antonio Bellini. It turned out that his family was descended from nobility in Milan, where they owned several vineyards. His wife was indeed, very understanding Ernesta had told me earlier.

It was my fervent hope that Italian women were better at it than I had been, and that they suffered less abuse. I put Signore Bellini out of my mind and slept very well that night.

Another bouquet of flowers was delivered to my room. These were red roses with yellow lilies and they were as beautiful as the previous flowers, though in a different color combination. *Maybe he's trying to figure out which kind I prefer,* I thought. Despite the flowers in Livorno, we had returned to Roma. My other thought was, *How had he found the little <u>pensione</u> where we're staying?*

Carrying the bouquet down the hall to the kitchen, I found a vase, put water in it, and deposited the flowers. *At supper that night I'll give them to our landlady.* Right now I was only concerned with getting Bess up and moving. We were going to Pompeii.

The lump of Bess in her bed reminded me of the lump in my mattress on which I had slept on all night. The good part about staying here, beside the price, was being in a residential neighborhood where I could practice my Italian and see ordinary people. I was getting tired of tour guides, taxi drivers, and waiters.

Every male in Roma thought that all American women were rich and promiscuous. Maybe we should write a guidebook for Italian men about American women.

"Bess, get up, please." This was the third time I tried to rouse the sleep deprived Bess and I was getting a little short of patience.

"I know that we haven't had much sleep, but we have to get going. Bess!"

"All right, I'm up." The pile of bedclothes didn't move.

"Bess!"

When the blankets actually moved, I went back to the kitchen to make a piece of toast and pour *espresso* into a small cup. Carrying it back to our room, I noticed that the lump had left the bed and was nowhere to be seen.

Once we were out the door we walked quickly to a bus stop and soon were headed to the train station. Taking the train allowed us to see the countryside out the window. I loved the informality of the Italian people, which was quite evident in their gardens along the railroad tracks. French gardens had been very orderly. Here they took more natural forms and looked happier, somehow. When we got off the train in Naples a tour guide stopped us to ask if we needed his services. I explained to him in Italian, that we didn't need a guide, today.

He was kind enough to point out that our jewelry could make us targets for thieves. He said that there were many poor people in Naples who would grab the jewelry from our necks and arms and sell it for bread. We removed all our jewelry and put it in the money belts under our clothes. Papa had made us get the money belts, saying that he didn't want us penniless in a foreign country.

When we got to Pompeii, Bess bought a map from the tourist bureau and we began walking through the ancient city. Many of the buildings had been restored to a state almost as good as the day that Vesuvius buried the town. We were a little appalled to find a tavern on every corner or at least it seemed that way. It had been a major seaport and sailors loved their grog. Since water of that time period was almost always contaminated, it was probably better for them to drink the mulled wine so favored by the citizens of Pompeii.

Happy with our tourist status we hoped to find a place that appealed to us near Pompeii, so that we could rent a small villa and settle in for a time. Viewing the remains of the ancient world was educational and walking was good for us, but we wanted to learn more about the people and culture of Italy. It kept me involved, able to avoid obsessing about why we were in Europe.

I had my nose in our guidebook when I heard a familiar voice.

"Ah, Signora Violetta." He was grinning from ear to ear and Bess was smiling, too.

"The housekeeper at your *pensione* told me where you had gone. How are you this day?" Taking a step forward he stretched out his hand and automatically I extended mine to shake his, but he took my gloved hand and lifted it to his lips.

"Signore Bellini. I am well, but please don't send any more flowers. The pollen is bad for my allergies. But thank you for the thought." Maybe that would give him pause before he sent any more.

"Signora Galland was just telling me that you are quite taken with Pompeii."

"I am, but we have to keep moving, Signore Bellini. I only have one day left before we leave for M..." I caught myself in time and said, "For Assisi."

"What a shame. I had hoped to escort the pair of you around Roma. I am an excellent guide and my fee is very small. Only that you both have dinner with me."

"Oh, that would be heavenly, Signore. Violet and I were hoping to see the catacombs and the buses are so irregular out there. Have you a motorcar?" Bess was genuinely pleased, and was thinking that there was no way out of it.

"Motorcar? What is this?"

"She means an automobile."

"Oh, Si. Si. It is quite near here. I would be delighted to take you back to Roma and escort you wherever you wish to go."

"Violet, we can visit the Museum and then go with Antonio. Come on, let's go."

On the train the next day, I was grateful that we had gone with Antonio. We had seen twice as much as we would have been able to see by bus, and had a wonderful dinner at a little sidewalk café. The veal Parmesan was excellent and we had loved the chocolate torte that they had been served for dessert. Even my feet were happy as we left the café. Probably, I had drank a bit more than my share of wine, but my feet did not complain of the day of seeing the sights.

The next morning, Antonio came to pick us up and take us to the train station. As he was opening the boot of his car, I noticed two suitcases already in it. It turned out that he was returning to Milan and would share his first class compartment with us until he got off in Milan and then we could continue to use it as we traveled on to Assisi.

Of course, he tried very hard to be charming, and asked repeatedly that we stop over a few days in Milan so that he could show us around.

I tried to decline, ever so sweetly, though I was tempted to say to him that I would very much have liked to meet his wife.

When he finally got off the train, I reached for my favorite little pillow, and hit Bess over the head repeatedly for encouraging him. Oh, what fun we were having! It felt so good.

From Milan, we visited Assisi, Padua, and Venice, before returning to Naples, as we would be looking for our villa between there and Pompeii. Declining invitations politely, almost every day, we looked forward to resting for a time, on the west coast of Italy.

Chapter XXIV

In Kansas, I knew that the winter temperatures must be causing problems for the farmers and ranchers, but in Rome the temperature was warm, very warm.

Standing on the balcony I looked out into the courtyard below and saw flowers blooming. The walls of the building were a golden ivory and seemed to radiate heat. The tiles below were terra cotta. It seemed that the Italians fought the lower temperatures of winter with the warmth of the earth.

And their hearts were also warm. I had never spent time among such a heartily kind people. Everywhere that I spoke their language, they were quick to accept me and help me. Guides weren't necessary for me. I didn't feel like a foreigner. Not anymore.

In my hand was a postcard from Enrico and I thought it the best New Year's greeting that I had ever received. It had pudgy little cupids on the front and very few words on the back:

Mia Cara
Buono giorno. Buono anno.
Et al da il fuo
                Enrico

Signora Violetta Murdock
             ROMA

Such a lovely note, "My Heart, Good Day…Good Year…From Your Enrico"

Despite all my resolutions, I had met a man that I could love, yet I was surprised and afraid of getting hurt. The Isle of Capri would forever seem a fairyland to me, the place where I had met Enrico and found that I could love again.

Bess and I had been invited to visit friends in Italy for Christmas. Bess had found an entertaining companion and was headed for the Alps for some skiing, and "snuggling" by the fireplace. So, I had gone to Capri, alone. I stood looking down into the courtyard of a grand villa. Definitely beyond my means, I was inspired to look even harder for the right courtyard, the right tile roof, and the warmest of seaside cliffs. If it weren't for my parents, I would never have gone home.

The postcard had been slipped under my door, and was still in my hand as I greeted the New Year from the balcony. I would carry it in my purse, later, when we went to St Peter's for Mass.

For months, I had avoided becoming too familiar with any man. I had been so hurt by Roland.

I held onto that marriage for years, waiting, praying for the happiness that all young women want and need. Despite my mother's disapproval, I had finally divorced him.

I had hardened my heart and stayed away from the charming men that I had met on the boat, coming over. I hadn't accepted any overtures from handsome Italian men or courtly Frenchmen, and certainly had not been impressed with the hand-kissing, heel-clicking German sojourners in Italy.

I had been so careful, yet Enrico had gotten past all my defenses.

Walks in the moonlight, champaign dinners, sightseeing, and his wit and expertise at the card table hadn't done it. No, it was his consistent thoughtfulness of me.

He hadn't rushed me, never expected anything, and was unfailingly courteous. Enrico had seen that I had been hurt. He would sit and listen to me, holding my hand, providing a handkerchief when appropriate, and never taking my reticence lightly. He had been very patient and slowly over the past two weeks, I had stepped closer to that cliff.

If I fell this time, if I hit bottom again, I didn't think that I would ever be able to get back up.

The doors to St. Peter's Basilica were huge, but in winter, smaller side doors were used in order to keep the temperature inside comfortable for the visitors. On an overcast day, the light in the huge cathedral was low, yet everything sparkled. Even the giant bronze columns of the canopy of the main altar had glints of gold where the stylized leaves had been polished. I stood in the enormous nave and slowly turned in one spot. It was hard to look up at the copula, it was so high. Enrico had promised to take me up inside. He had said that the view from the top of St. Peter's was unsurpassed. At the base of the copula I could see carvings, beautiful paintings, and everywhere there was gold leaf. The most beautiful stained glass window in this complex, multi-faceted jewel of a church was the Holy Spirit window. The white dove hung in a field of yellow and gold, the glass panes cut into rays that flowed from the Spirit. The window moldings were elaborate with carvings and golden rays beaming around the glowing window. The window was simple, yet the frame was rich in detail and expression of form and line. At that one moment, I wished that I were Catholic, yet I knew that I would never leave the Episcopal Church. I thought of the postcard in my purse and smiled. I felt Enrico's hand on my elbow and looked at him.

"Come, let's go into the crypt where the early Popes are buried. Hadrian's tomb is there. He built many of the fortifications of the city, including Castel de Angeli.

"As a soldier, I always like to greet him when I visit St. Peter's." I let my self be led to the doorway that would take us to the stairs under the massive basilica, and followed him down the marble staircase. In the dim light of the crypt, I saw many sarcophagi holding the bones of former popes. Here were the rulers, not only of Vatican City, because at one time their power had been felt as far away as England and Asia Minor.

Enrico delighted in telling me the stories of the popes, and then took me to the Sistine Chapel where the greatness of Michelangelo shone as a bright light in Italian Art. And then we visited two museums within the walls of the Vatican. Everywhere were the relics of the past. Embroidered capes, jeweled papal tiaras, reliquaries, gold bound books, and weapons belonging to the troops that once fought to keep the Vatican secure.

My mother saved magazines and souvenirs for years. I had thought Momma a bit silly for keeping bits of ribbon and paper. Looking at the treasures of the Church, some of them 1900 years old and still in serviceable condition, I marveled at the care and attention needed to do this.

Later, we heard Mass together. My Italian was becoming so good that I understood much of the Italianated Latin. I especially loved the hymns, some of which we had sung in my own church. I wondered about the lives of the people who had kept those songs alive for a thousand years before my church had even been born.

Enrico and I went to lunch in a beautiful restaurant. We had cannelloni and for dessert, of course, gelato. The wine warmed me. We walked to the Trevi fountain, which was dry for the winter, but still a great work of art. I was glad that he loved works of Art, as I did.

The New Year was here and I felt that I could begin again, but cautiously, carefully. Enrico was so understanding, so gentle, so much in love with me. I could see it in his eyes.

In the carriage, with Enrico's arm around me I relaxed while the coachman drove us out of Rome to see more of the many ruins. There was quiet strength in his arms and I felt safe.

"Violetta, I want you to come to my mother's estate in the countryside near Assisi. It is very beautiful and the people are warm hearted, it isn't as warm there, but I promise to keep you warm." He smiled into my eyes then kissed me tenderly on the forehead.

I looked into those brown eyes and couldn't see how I could refuse to visit his mother's home.

"Are you sure that you want to introduce me to your mother, Enrico? Don't you think it's a bit soon?"

"That isn't a problem. My mother will not be there. She has gone to Monaco for two months."

"So, there isn't anyone there?"

"Just the servants. We can be alone, Mia Cara." He raised my hand to his lips, still looking into my eyes.

"I don't think that's a good idea. I have been under scrutiny since my divorce and I don't want to encourage tongues to wag."

"But no one will know, Violetta, and if they did, they would not care. We are both adults.

"What could anyone say?"

"They could say that I have no morals. They can write to my parents and upset them. I won't have anymore talk about me; I won't!"

A few days later we went to Pompeii where I wanted to rent a small villa for a year, or more. On a small hill north of the little town was a ten-room house in the ever-present cream color, but inside it was bright with light and color. Every room was drenched in sunlight and the shutters on the windows were bright blue. The fireplaces were tiled in every hue of the rainbow. The kitchen was on the east side of the house and I knew that it would be a welcome sight on a winter morning.

I was enchanted and wanted it immediately, but Enrico asked me to wait a few days so that he could check into the owners and the price seemed a little high to him. I liked that he wanted to help me in obtaining the house of my dreams, so allowed him to handle the securing of the little villa.

A week later I received a letter with the terms of the agreement and a lease for me to sign. There was also a note from Enrico that everything was in order and he had even found a woman to cook and clean for me.

The rent was substantially lower than I had expected. I was very excited and when Enrico came to pick me up to go to the opera, I thanked him repeatedly. He denied giving any money to the owners of the villa, so I wasn't sure that my rent had been lowered because of that or because Enrico had gotten the owner to take less money. I didn't care.

That evening we attended the opera, and afterwards dined at sweet little café near the opera house. I drank several Irish coffees and talked about the opera, life, and my growing affection for him.

In the carriage, I leaned against him and thought of my upcoming move to Pompeii. Would he come so far to see me?

When the carriage stopped, he helped me down and walked me to the door that led into the courtyard of the *pensione* where I was staying. When he unlocked it for me, he stepped through and took me into his arms. His lips were soft but urgent and I responded.

It was late and I had had too much wine, and then coffee laced with whiskey. I felt warm and so safe. He kissed me more deeply and I slid my arms under his cape and around his waist. Leaning into him, my lips parted and became softer, drawing him into me.

A wave of passion swept over me. All the months of loneliness, the hurt of the divorce, the feelings of abandonment, of being unloved.

Enrico obviously loved me and I couldn't keep pushing him away. I didn't want to push him away any longer. The feelings couldn't be kept in, I needed to feel loved, to feel desirable, as I hadn't felt for so long.

Enrico pulled back. His hands were on my arms, gently pushing me back.

"Mia Cara, if you don't stop, I will die right here, right now. It's late and I think you had a little too much to drink."

Now, he held my hands, looking down at me in the muted light of a lantern by the door.

"I will come for you tomorrow and drive you to your new home.

"Until tomorrow, sleep well, my darling," and he kissed my hands and left me.

Almost staggering, from the drink, from the passion, I moved to the stairs and climbed to my room. After this night, I knew that I couldn't ever stop his lovemaking, again, and I didn't want to stop him or myself.

Holding hands Enrico and I walked through the gardens of his mother's country estate. Towering Yew trees and the ever-present Poplars cast long shadows across the rolling, green lawn. Flowering vines grew on the marble columns and lintels made to look like the ancient remains of a Roman temple to Aphrodite. Cascading grapevines covered the pergola and I admired the deep purple of the grapes, just approaching full ripeness. But it was as though I walked in a dream, surrounded by such beauty, yet I was numb.

The statue of the goddess of love smiled down on us and I felt a pang of regret. I remembered how much I had loved Roland, how beautiful his eyes were, and how high my hopes had been. There were no hopes this time.

Enrico was to be married, but not to me. I had received a telegram from Bess that morning. She had seen the engagement announcement in the newspaper that morning. He had never said a word. Not one word. How could he have deceived me so?

"Mia Cara, of what are you thinking?" His dark brown eyes were soft in the shade of the pergola. In sunlight they sometimes glittered like the jet beads that my grandmother had favored.

"Have I been misinformed or are you to be married two weeks from now?" I asked, the hurt obviously apparent. My voice was quiet, sad. I turned away from him resting my hand on the warm marble column and looked toward the villa where a fountain sent jets of water into the air to come down on an endearing statue of Pan playing his pipes.

"Violetta, we will always be together."

"That's a lovely sentiment, Enrico, but there isn't any future for us. You will marry someone named Francesca, of whom you have told me nothing, and I will go back to Pompeii, alone. " My hands reached out to pluck at a dead leaf on the grapevine nearest me. The leaf was becoming brittle in the heat and I started breaking small pieces off of it and throwing them as far as I could, but being very light and not aerodynamic in shape, they fell rapidly to the ground in front of me. I stepped on them and ground them into the earth.

"I don't see any reason for me to stay here. I think I'll pack and leave for Rome, tonight, Enrico." There was hurt and anger in my voice. "Please tell your man to drive me to the train station this evening."

I would have walked away then, but his arms closed around me, turning me to face him. His arms strong, holding me tightly against him.

"Please, Violetta, don't leave tonight. I can't bear it if you go away when you are so angry. With anxiety in his voice, he spoke softly and he held me tightly.

"Enrico, let go of me. I will not be forced to do anything – not ever, again." Shoving against his chest, I struggled to create some space between us. He let me step back a few inches, but didn't release me.

"What does it matter that I am forced into this marriage? My parents can tell me who to marry, but not who to love. I love you, Violetta. Only you."

"Let go of me." I looked into his eyes and he could see that I was angry. Twisting in his arms, I lashed out with a fist and hit him hard enough to hurt him.

"I have been forced to marry, too, Enrico, by circumstance and by parents, but I made a commitment and I tried very hard to make it work.

"You talk as though you are being forced to join a play or a baseball team. And what of the poor woman? Is she free to have other relationships or will she be as I was, desperately trying to create a true, Christian marriage?"

"Mia Cara," he reached toward me and I backed away.

"No! I will not treat her as I was treated. I will not encourage you in your infidelities.

"If I had known that you were engaged, I would never have... have..."

A great sob made me bow at the waist and I covered my face with my hands. His strong hands touched my shoulders and I leapt away from him, as though his palms had burnt my flesh.

Pulling a lace-trimmed handkerchief from the waistband of my linen dress, I wiped my tears, and then hurried down the shade of the pergola. My heels hit the marble walk with determination and grew faster with each step until I was almost running.

Inside the villa, I again wiped the tears from my eyes as I walked as calmly as I could up the pink marble staircase. My eyes touched lightly on the beautiful statues in their niches, and the large urns carved with cherubs, grapes, and vines. Everything was so splendid, but my heart was ruined. I had been so sure that he loved me. He was a man of the world, had a Master's Degree in Literature, spoke eight languages fluently and had traveled to every part of the world. He knew politics, but had no political ambition. He had studied Theology, but never considered a career in the Church. He had worked in his uncle's import/export business, but had no need of money.

In all things, he was independent, yet he would not go against his family's wishes.

He had sworn to support me, love, and care for me the rest of my life, but he never had any intention of marrying me. I thought that he was being faithful to me, sharing his life with me. In his mind he was showing his devotion to me.

I looked at it from a more American/Puritanical viewpoint.

If you really love someone, you marry him. If you are committed, you do not have a mistress, however "European" you might be.

Grabbing my suitcase from the closet in my room, I began opening drawers and taking piles of silken undergarments out of the dresser. With little regard for wrinkles or organization I started transferring them to my suitcase.

A timid looking maid came in and quietly began to help. It was a few moments before I even noticed that the girl was there, then I stepped aside and let her take over.

"Madam."

I turned toward the maid, who spoke to me in broken English.

"Signore Enrico asked if you could please speak with him in the library." She looked very earnest and I thought for a moment.

"I will speak to him. Finish my packing and order the car." I spoke in a firm voice and my most formal Italian, turned and walked out of the room.

Holding my head high, I walked down the stairs and went to the double doors of the library. I paused for a moment then took hold of the handles and opened both doors in one sweep. Leaving them open I stepped into the large library that had hints of French Empire in the furniture and architecture.

He stood at the window.

"You wished to say something to me, Enrico?"

Somewhere in my Victorian heart, I still hoped that he would choose me over the wishes of his family or the rulings of his Church. There was a tiny spark inside me, the smallest glimmer of hope that I would be loved as I had never been loved. Totally. Unconditionally.

Standing straight and tall, I waited.

Surely he loved me enough. He had to love me enough. I had done everything I could to show my devotion to him, even giving into his love making, believing he would love me enough to marry me.

Enrico calmly turned toward me, and I saw his charm, his affection in the look he gave me.

"Violetta, you are being foolish. I have a generous income and can give you a beautiful apartment in Rome, Milan, even in Florence. Or if you wish, I will buy you one of those charming little places on Capri.

"I can give you a good income and spend much time with you. I love you. Please, give me a chance." There was a note of pleading in his voice. He was trying to explain things to me, as though I hadn't understood him before.

"You didn't mention Venice, Enrico. Will you offer to get me a place in Venice?"

"I would, if I could, Violetta. But I can't seem to flaunt you in front of my wife and family."

"I cannot believe this! I told you from the start I had been treated poorly by my husband. I was abused, neglected, and abandoned. I told you that I would never allow myself to be treated poorly again, and you stand there and ask me to allow you to do it to me. Once again, what about Kohler?

"No. I'm not going to be treated so. And if you were a true man, you would not do it to me or to your fiancée. Stay away from me, Enrico. If you try to see me or call me I will refuse you.

"If you continue to harass me, I will speak to your parents or to Francesca. Do you understand me?" I became aware of a sharp pain, and realized that my nails were cutting into the palms of my hands. I was furious at him, but punishing myself. Consciously relaxing my fists, I waited until he nodded, then turned and climbed the stairs, again.

By this time, my trunk had been brought to my room and there were two maids packing my things. I saw my traveling dress hanging in the closet.

"Please draw a bath for me and finish packing while I bathe.

"Do you know when the train to Rome leaves?"

"At eight this evening, Signora. Shall I reserve a drawing room for you?"

"Si."

I sat down at the vanity and looked at my hair. It was still in a romantic pompadour style, when Bess had already adopted a shorter, easier cut for style and ease of care. I decided to get a hair cut when I reached Rome. I needed a change in my life and a new hair cut was a start. I had a few more months on my lease on the house in Pompeii. When it lapsed I would go to Paris and visit friends I had met while in Europe.

I would never give my heart, again. Never. That was a firm resolution. No more Rolands or Enricos. No more pain

Chapter XXV

My resolve to never fall in love again failed me in the spring of 1914. Through friends of mine in Independence, Kansas, I met Jerome Kohler. Jerome was in Independence visiting his brother, and we were introduced. I already knew his wife. We had met while attending the same social club a few years before.

Jerome was an intense man, with a quick wit, and keen intelligence. It was said he was descended from a noble family in Switzerland, though he reminded me of the German men I had met when in Europe. He was reluctant to speak of his family or his heritage, only that he was a successful businessman in Los Angeles.

It was a beautiful spring evening and I had been invited to Independence for a barbeque at the home of some friends. The lilacs were in bloom and their scent filled the backyard, as did the honeysuckle that grew all along the fence. The day had been mild and the evening was gorgeous.

It felt good to be back home in Kansas. I had loved being abroad, but my parents were getting older, and they had missed me terribly while I was gone, so I knew I was where I should be. Papa and I had been trying to figure out what I should do with my life and we had discussed that I might go back to school. I had always been a good student, and, Lord knew, I needed some kind of structure in my life. I had made the decision to go back to school in the fall, but I hadn't decided where yet. Just having made the decision was enough for me at the moment. Spring and summer were always filled with things to do, parties to attend, so I wasn't worried about becoming bored too soon.

A few days after the party, there was a knock at the front door. Lemon came to the library, where I had been reading, and informed me I had a caller. I walked to the front door and there was Jerome

Kohler, standing in the carriage entryway, smiling at me. I couldn't imagine what in the world he would be doing at the mansion. *Did I leave something at the party?* The thought flitted through my mind.

I extended my hand toward him in greeting, and then asked if he would like to sit down. Lemon came back in and offered to get us something to drink. After a few moments of formal conversation, I couldn't help but come right out and ask what he was doing here.

"Mr. Kohler, if you'll excuse me for asking, what is the purpose of your visit today?" I asked rather boldly, and then hoped I hadn't sounded rude.

"Well, Mrs. Murdock, I don't quite know, to be honest. I know I should have called first, asked if it was all right to come out. I don't know...I just wanted to see you again." He said sheepishly.

"I'm not sure I understand what you mean." I was beginning to grow more uncomfortable by the moment. *What in the world?* I pondered.

Lemon walked into the parlor at that moment with tall glasses of lemonade and a small china plate of cookies. She set the tray down on the table in front of me, so that I could serve my guest, and then she quietly left the room.

My anxiety level was increasing by the moment. I knew instinctively that this visit wasn't a good idea, but the "why" of it had me quite intrigued. I hadn't spoken more than briefly with Mr. Kohler the night we met at the party. He was very handsome, that was true, but he was also very married, and that was all I needed to know to make me turn and walk the other direction. But, why had he come here?

"Do you mind if I address you by your first name, Mrs. Murdock?" he asked.

"I really don't see the purpose..." I began.

"I know this is confusing," he interrupted, "But if you'll only let me explain maybe you'll understand a little better. Maybe we'll both understand a little better." He went on rather reluctantly. "I've thought about you since the night of the party, and haven't quite been able to get you off my mind. I hope that doesn't shock you, but it's the truth. I was hoping, maybe, that we could get to know each other better." He smiled hesitantly and looked quite embarrassed.

"Mr. Kohler, I'm sorry if this sounds rude, but you're a married man. I really don't understand the reason for this visit." I answered.

"I know we've just met and you don't know anything about me," he explained. "My life is quite complicated that's true. Yes, I am a married man, but not a happily married one. I've been wanting to leave my wife for quite some time now, and have made the decision to do so." Meekly, he added, "I was hoping we could become friends."

I was stunned into silence. I felt my mouth drop open and am sure I had quite a dazed look on my face. I didn't know what to say.

Finally, I gained my equilibrium and spoke. "Mr. Kohler, I appreciate your honesty, truly I do, but I really don't find this to be appropriate behavior at all. I think you should leave."

"You're right," he answered, rising as he spoke. "Of course, you're right. I don't know what I was thinking coming here. Please forgive me."

He turned to walk out of the parlor and then stopped and faced me once again.

"I am filing for a divorce from my wife. If it's all right, I will contact you again soon, and see if you've changed your mind about getting to know each other."

With that said, he walked out through the front door and quietly closed it behind him.

"What in the world just happened here?" I exclaimed to the empty room.

In the weeks to come, Jerome pursued me relentlessly. He called, he wrote letters, he even sent flowers. One evening about three weeks later I agreed to dinner. Of course we had to dine in another town for fear of gossip, but it was worth the drive. We talked about our lives, our disappointments, the parts that had been good, and the parts that had been painful. I confided in him things I thought I would never share with a man again. He was so sincere and thoughtful, understanding and comforting. I had mixed emotions about seeing him as he was still a married man, but he convinced me not to worry about that as well.

This man had just appeared in my life out of the blue and swept me off my feet. I couldn't have been more surprised and pleased at my good fortune. I tried to keep my friendship with Jerome a secret from Momma and Papa, but, of course, they figured it out what with the letters coming daily, phone calls, and flowers. Momma was horrified that I would even consider such a risk to my reputation, and was quite vocal about her disapproval. Papa, on the other hand, told me in private to do what my heart led me to do and he would keep Momma out of the way. He knew how lonely I was and it broke his heart. I was still a young woman; only twenty-eight. I decided to throw caution to the wind and see what happened. It felt good to receive attention again from a handsome man, and after all, he was in the process of divorce, I reasoned to myself.

When he asked me to marry him that summer, I accepted. We planned a quiet affair and were married by the Justice of the Peace in Independence. We both felt it would be better to have the marriage performed with as little fuss as possible. After the ceremony, we left for the East coast for our honeymoon. We would then travel to Los Angeles, where Jerome wanted us to make our home.

Papa had construction begun on a house in town as a wedding gift. It was a two-story bungalow on a corner lot. This way, Papa reasoned, we would have our own private residence when we came home to Coffeyville for visits. It wasn't even finished when the marriage fell apart. Within six months of marrying Jerome, this charming, romantic man who had romanced me and won my heart had turned into a stranger. He became rude and inattentive. I began to have the overwhelming emotions of my first marriage. Once again, I had gone into a relationship with the hope that it would be different this time; that I couldn't be this unlucky, this cursed. Papa was the one who finally told me what he had feared all along. Jerome had believed my family to be wealthier than his own, and he had thought that he could have an easy life, not having to work or use his own money to finance any of his dreams of instant success, using my father as his banker. He was paying his ex-wife a small fortune each month, and reminded me often, he was doing it to keep her from blackmailing me because of our affair. She had threatened to take me to court for alienating her husband's affections, but she never did. I always wondered if Papa had a hand in that situation, but never had the nerve to just ask him.

What had I gotten myself into this time? How could I have been so naïve to think any man could truly love me or be committed to only me?

One day he just disappeared. At the end of twelve months, I filed for divorce and asked for nothing. I existed in a state of disbelief.

I'm through trying, God. I'm through. I'm worn out from it. There will be no more men for me, not ever. Don't put one in my path tomorrow or next year, or the year after that, for I will veer so far from him as to completely lose my sanity in the process. I'm hanging on by a thread here, a mere thread. How could I have been such a fool, again.

No amount of berating myself eased my troubled heart. The only thing that saved my life was staying true to the decision to return to school, get my degree, and move forward the best I possibly could. It was the only choice I had.

Chapter XXVI

By 1932, it was necessary for me to come back to Coffeyville. Both my parents were in poor health and they needed me to help care for them. My father's ulcer disease was causing him constant discomfort, and my mother had health problems as well. They were both in their early seventies.

I had been living in Ponca City, Oklahoma. After the divorce from Jerome, I went back to school and obtained my Library of Science degree. I found a job in Ponca City, as a librarian and loved it. My world was books from morning until night.

I came home from Ponca City feeling somewhat reluctant. I had made a life for myself and was finally starting to feel as though I belonged somewhere. I had made friends and liked my job. It was with a sense of duty that I returned home, hoping that maybe it would be a temporary situation and that Momma and Papa would somehow return to good health. That was not to be. Momma had been in a state of depression for over twenty years and it had taken a toll on her health. Her eating habits were poor and it had been a constant battle for years to get her to take care of herself. She had simply lost her will to live after Donald died. After his death, she continued to work in the greenhouse and help Papa occasionally with his businesses from his office at the mansion, but there was no gaiety or merriment in the house.

While Donald was still alive, she had developed facial pain and this had become more severe over the years. It was pain that was seizure-like with spasms of the nerve that would last from a few seconds to a few minutes at a time and would occur spontaneously throughout the day. The pain of these spasms was horrid to endure. By 1932, it was determined the pain was caused by the trigeminal nerve, and all three branches were affected. Momma was on constant doses of pain- relieving medications. Her once beautiful face was stricken with a paralysis on one side, which made it difficult for her to eat, even when she had an appetite. She continually fought kidney infections, as well because she would not drink enough fluids; therefore, her days were filled with pain.

My father's ulcer disease had progressed to the point of seeking help at the Mayo Clinic where he would return quite often in the last two years of his life. Even though, Lemon kept him on a strict diet of bland foods, nothing seemed to help, and he had many days that were filled with pain and discomfort.

Mama and Papa had gone steadily downhill and I was needed, it was as simple as that. They had been so good to me over the course of my lifetime, and I felt guilty about their illnesses being an interruption in my life. I had a firm talk with myself as I made the drive home and decided I would do everything I could to be a comfort to my parents.

My days were filled with helping Lemon to care for them and make them as comfortable as possible. I helped Momma in the greenhouse when she felt like working there and read to them both in the evenings. By this time, we had our own radio station in Coffeyville, KGGF, and they enjoyed listening to the radio shows in the evenings as well. I would go to bed exhausted, but feeling like I had been a genuine help to them. With their health like it was, there was little in their lives, and Momma had basically sealed herself off from life in Coffeyville. She didn't really care to receive visitors and had become quite reclusive. Her life was Papa and her greenhouse. There were always arrangements of fresh flowers in the house, filling it up with their sweet scent of the season. Papa had begun to raise Airedales and Scotties after he became semi-retired and the dogs gave him pleasure. The Airedales made excellent watchdogs. The Scotties were his favorite.

I had been away for quite some time when I came home to live in 1932. I joined the library board in town and began to make new friends with whom I would play bridge once or twice a week and I read a lot when I wasn't caring for my parents. The Natatorium was still in operation, but the spa had been closed for years by then. I would go to the pool occasionally and have a swim, and that would refresh me after a long day of nursing my parents.

I have fond memories of the friends I made during that period of my life. They became friends that I would share time with from that point on. I've never forgotten how Catherine Chapman Read and Frances Read Kaiser would do their best to help me find time for myself in the midst of caring for my parents. The times I spent with them and their young niece, Mary Maud Read, were happy times. Catherine and I taught young Mary Maud how to swim at the Natatorium when she was young. She would tease Catherine and I because we would never allow our faces to touch the water for fear of them turning black.

I also made a good friend in Jessie Zeigler. She had lived a very interesting life. Her mother had been a singer at the Perkins Opera House when Jessie was a young girl, and had been accompanied by the very well known pianist, Blind Boone. Jessie's mother later married a wealthy banker from Independence, who had been at the opera house one evening and heard her mother sing. He requested an introduction after her performance, and after a time they had married.

By the spring of 1934, we knew my father wouldn't live much longer. Doctors had done all they could do at Mayo, and we could only keep him comfortable until the end. He became extremely ill on a Sunday night in June, with pain and nausea. By the following morning his body had gone into shock and he died of a massive hemorrhage of the stomach.

My mother, even though my father's death was expected, was devastated. She couldn't bear the thought of life without him. I made all the funeral arrangements and even had to choose the casket in which he would be buried. We held the funeral at home and then he was transported to Elmwood Cemetery to be buried in the family plot with the boys.

My mother gave up completely after that; she just felt there was no point in trying to go on any longer. She refused to eat, and would not accept liquids. Her will to live was gone. I admitted her to the Southeast Kansas Hospital on August 3rd. On my last visit with her, she pulled me close so she could whisper in my ear.

"Violet, I have to go be with Papa. You understand don't you, honey? I love you, my Violet." Her voice was a whisper with long pauses between each statement and I strained to hold onto every word wanting to remember each one. She was so weak and her tiny body so worn out from her lifetime of losses. As strong as my Mama had always been, there had been so much loss that she couldn't prevent... losing Donald and then losing Papa. I shook my head in acknowledgement to let her know that I understood that she loved me, but needed to be with Papa. I held her even tighter. I didn't want her to see my tears as I thought of letting her go.

She followed my father on August 25, 1934, dying of complications due to blood clots and kidney failure. As I had done just two months before, I arranged her funeral and had her laid to rest next to my father.

My family was gone. At forty-nine years of age, I had buried both of my brothers, my father and my mother. I had tried so hard to keep my parents alive, but there was nothing I could do but watch as their illnesses took over their bodies. These were the two people I loved most in the world and now they were gone. They had given me everything I had ever wanted. Now I was to face the world alone. They had tried to prepare me as best they could, but the loneliness at their passing was incomparable to anything I had ever experienced. I turned away everyone who tried to comfort me. I wanted no comfort, no company. Looking back over the years of my life all I could see was one loss after another, one disappointment after another. How was I to live the rest of my life? The mansion had been left to me, but there was no solace in that. I was left financially comfortable, but it offered me no peace.

As I had done in the past, I turned to my books for comfort. I lost myself in the stories I read, one book after the other, for days on end. I had entered my parents' bedroom the afternoon of my mother's funeral, straightened it, pulled down the shades, and closed the door. I would not enter the room again, nor would I allow any of the servants to enter it. I wanted it left completely as it was. My mother had closed the door to Donald's room twenty years before and only she had been allowed to go in. I was accustomed to closed doors now. Maybe someday I would open them back up, but not now, not yet. I would give myself some time to grieve, some time to mourn. Then, perhaps, one day, I would consider opening the doors to the rooms of my loved ones, pull up the shades, and let the rays of the sun shine in them once again – maybe, someday.

Chapter XXVII

After the death of my parents, I slowly settled back into the familiar habits of small town life. I missed them terribly and the house seemed too big, too quiet, too empty. I had become accustomed to long days and nights of caring for my sick mother and father. Now, I had too much time on my hands.

Times were tough in the mid-1930s. After the crash of 1929, Coffeyville had difficulty getting back on its feet. It had left people without jobs, no way to pay their rent, and two and three families would live in one home to try to make ends meet. A canning factory opened with the help of the W.P.A. program, and jobs were provided for several hundred people. When the Second World War started in 1938, Coffeyville was still under hard times and farmers were losing their homes and farms.

There was a reprieve from the gloomy situation when the summer of 1940 rolled around. Every conversation in every part of town centered on the Hollywood motion picture production of, "When the Dalton's Rode."

Emmett Dalton had been paroled in 1907, pardoned by the Governor of the State of Kansas. He wrote a book while still imprisoned, entitled, "Beyond the Law" which told the story of his daring days as an outlaw. The book was published in 1918. The wounds he had received during the robbery of the two banks would remind him forever of his wrongdoing. He never completely healed from his injuries and had to have more than one restorative operation. He and Dr. Wells, the doctor who had saved his life, had stayed in contact with each other over the years, and not only corresponded in written form, but exchanged gifts as well. Emmett had been so young when the raid occurred, and had primarily been forgiven for his part in what had transpired on that beautiful fall day in 1892. He had served over fifteen years in prison and the governor felt his debt had been paid.

The movie, "When the Dalton's Rode" would have its world premiere here in town and the movie stars from Hollywood were coming. Committees were formed by the Historical Society and plans were underway for a huge celebration. There would be a parade with everyone dressed in period clothing and the town would be draped in 1890s style. Everyone who had a wagon, cowboy outfit, guns, horses, furniture, any relic of the past, was asked to lend it to the festivities. Young women, who were employed at Coffeyville businesses, would have the opportunity to play hostess to the movie stars after their arrival to town. By the middle of July, everyone's thoughts focused on this event.

I invited my friend, Bess, down from Wichita, for the premiere. We needed a good visit as it had been awhile since we'd seen each other. She came in on the train the day before the movie premiered. I picked her up and brought her out to the mansion where we talked nonstop late into the night, catching each other up on our lives. The memories we had made in Europe had bonded us together in a friendship that was as close as sisters. We giggled like teenage girls when reminiscing on our escapades. Oh, what a time that had been, until my heart had been broken, yet again.

The premiere was scheduled for July 25, 1940. Five of the movie stars arrived that day at the Missouri-Pacific train station; Randolph Scott, Frank Albertson, Andy Devine, Peggy Moran, Constance Moore, and director, George Marshall. They were taken from the station to the Dale Hotel, where they would rest until the festivities began.

Over 25,000 people were at the parade that day. They took up every square inch of available space there was to see the movie stars from Hollywood, as they rode in the latest automobiles down Eighth Street towards the Plaza. The actors addressed the crowd at the Plaza and showed true excitement at being able to take part in Coffeyville's historical past.

The premiere took place at two of the town's movie theatres that evening, the Midland Theatre and the Tackett. Admission was 35 cents. The theatres were packed. After the movie there was a dance at the Memorial Hall. It was truly a wonderful day for everyone, young and old, rich and poor. The Dalton raid was part of our history and it was a history we were proud of. The citizens of Coffeyville showed courage and bravery at a moment's notice, some lost their lives as a result, but the message had gone out regardless; there would be no raids on our banks without a fight. These brave people who lost their lives were the backbone of our town, heroes in every sense of the word, and to this day have never been forgotten. Sweet memories came back to me of Mama and Papa and his bravery during the raid. And it seemed, for a moment, that I could even feel the pain of my bruised and bloody feet when I had run after Momma trying desperately not to lose sight of her in the frantic crowd.

The furnace-like heat of summer finally transformed into the blessed cool of fall. Wendell Wilkie decided to run on the Republican ticket for President of the United States. This also caused much excitement here in Coffeyville, as Mr. Wilkie, had taught history at our high school during 1914 and 1915 and was very familiar to the townspeople, and to my own family as well. He began his speaking tour for the presidency right here with a history-making speech on September 15, 1940. The town was quite proud and this event allowed people to feel good about things, once again.

In 1943, Lemon decided it was time for her to think about retirement. She had worked long and hard over her lifetime and had been a faithful and devoted employee. She was more than that to my family and to me, especially. She decided it was her responsibility to find someone to replace her and promised me she wouldn't go until she had trained someone adequately to run the mansion. She found that person in a young woman who lived in the cluster of cottages across from the mansion. Papa had developed the land west of the mansion years before and had set up a neighborhood of small houses. More than one family who lived on these streets had worked at the mansion, as the accessibility to work was so convenient.

Mildred Schertz came to the mansion in response to the ad Lemon placed in *The Journal*. She was young, only nineteen years old, but very willing to learn the responsibilities Lemon had carried out for the last forty-nine years. Of course, it would be easier now as there was only one person to cook for, clean up after, and run errands for. Mildred was excited to take on the duties of the household. Lemon hired her and set about the task of teaching her what was to be expected from her. She stayed with me at the mansion until she felt secure about Mildred's ability and then retired to enjoy her family.

Neither of us would ever let too much time pass before getting together for tea and a catch-up conversation. Lemon never did get used to the fact that she wasn't the one who had to prepare things anymore, and usually wanted to fix the tea for us herself when she came out. I would sit at the kitchen table and watch her as she prepared tea and a snack, and as I would sit there, I would remind myself how graced I had been to have Lemon in my life.

Mildred not only became a skilled housekeeper, but over the years became a dear companion to me, as well.

But tragedy was not through with us yet, and in 1943, it visited us again with the death of Harry Gabler, Sophie's brother. In January, the coldest month of the year here in Kansas, he took his own life by drowning himself in the allegedly bottomless Shadow Lake. Another Gabler had taken his life. What had Valentine Gabler done to his son? Harry had seemed to do well in his adult life. He had married and even had a child of his own. He was a successful electrician. Yet, oddly though, he had lived in the garage apartment behind his childhood home at 702 W. 8th at forty-three years of age, even though he was married and had a child.

Valentine Gabler had been dead for years, having died at the age of sixty. He succumbed to a fatal heart attack in 1917, six years after the death of Sophie. He had gone to the doctor's office complaining of chest pain one morning and dropped dead in the waiting room. I thought it too easy a death for a man who had caused such great pain for an entire family.

Even after his death, his remaining daughters never left home. What a powerful hold this man had on his family, even from the grave. No one ever knew what haunted Harry Gabler's mind and what drove him to end his life in Shadow Lake. His wife and child left town shortly after the funeral and never returned.

What went on in that house of the Gabler family would forever remain a secret. Nor did I ever tell anyone of the horror of Sophie's life. Sophie's mother lived until 1935, when she died of heart related problems. To say that she knew nothing of the atrocities that occurred under her own roof would be like saying an owl doesn't know it can only see nocturnally. She knew something, how much or how little, no one will ever know. But she took that secret to the grave with her as well.

The Natatorium had become more trouble than it was worth and I was tired of the responsibility of holding onto it. It took more money to keep it running than it was bringing in, so after forty years of being a landmark in Coffeyville, it was sold. I made the decision to sell the Natatorium in 1947.

I also made another decision…in 1948. I decided it was time to go back to Machias. I took the money from the sale of the Nat, cashed in my war bonds, and went out East to choose a summer home for myself. I found it in Machiasport, just over the line from Machias. It was the oldest home in the whole area, built in 1776, by a man who had served in the first naval battle of the Revolutionary War in the Machias area. His name was Ebenezer Gardner. There was a family cemetery behind the house, where Ebenezer and his family rested. The house sat on fifty acres of woods and fields. The tidal stretch of the Machias River was spread before me from the front of the house, and the day I took possession I saw the rare sight of a bald eagle flying over the water as I stood on the porch for the first time as the owner.

I was back.

Within the next week, the seals, blue herons, and my favorite, the puffins, greeted me. The house was bought at Christmas time, so I decided I would spend Christmas there rather than another lonely holiday at the mansion. Mildred and I worked for two weeks getting the house decorated just as I wanted it.

Though I was sometimes exhausted, I went to bed happy at night. It brought back so many memories being there; memories of my family, of Roland. I had been so young then, so naïve. Things would be different this time around. I wasn't a young woman any longer. There would be no dances, no falling in love. That part of my life was over, and I had cried my last tears over that many years before. At least I thought I had.

The first night I saw the Quoddy Head Lighthouse blinking across the water, the tears came suddenly and flowed freely for the better part of an hour. I had fallen in love so deeply, so completely. Roland had caused me such pleasure and then had gone about creating the deepest wounds to my heart. Your brain isn't the only organ of the body that can hold the scars of a lifetime; the heart retains them as well. I cried openly and without shame that night, and then decided I would never cry over that period of my life again. Machias would only bring me happiness from that point on and I cherished my time spent there.

I spent months at a time at my new house. Springtime in Maine was gorgeous, with miles of land covered in white blossoms, blueberries in the summer, and the magnificent colors in the fall. Never had I seen trees turn so red, orange and russet.

My life there was quiet and serene. I enjoyed my books and was a regular visitor to the Porter Memorial Library. I had no interest in having any kind of social life. I was comfortable in my own skin by now and had come to terms years before with the fact that my life contained little more than myself for company. It was not to be for me to have the traditional life of husband and children. I had learned to live with it.

As Papa had said years before, "God gives, and God takes away." It was up to me to make my own happiness in this lifetime, and I was doing the best I possibly could. There were times when I was lonely, and only had my memories of a fuller life to give me comfort, but it was at those times I picked myself up and reminded myself that everyone has burdens, crosses to bear. If being alone was my cross, then I would do my best to fill my days with ways that would stimulate my brain, and my books did that. It was a quiet existence, to be sure, but there was never a more beautiful place than Machias to simply be quiet and take in the beauty that God had put on this earth.

I loved it there.

Chapter XXVIII

The 1950s were very prosperous times in Coffeyville. Houses were being built, businesses were opening, and the town was growing. People were happier than they had been in years. The next generation had been born, the Baby Boomers.

I had seen so many changes in my sixty-six years on this earth. I basically liked what I saw, but didn't feel a part of it, somehow. I lived an isolated existence at the mansion, by my own choice, but isolated just the same. I had bridge games with my friends to look forward to once a week, but, other than that, things were quiet. I still went to Machias for months at a time, but it was getting more difficult to manage two pieces of property. The expenses at the mansion were such that I had begun to get a little concerned by the late 1950s, early 1960s.

The mansion's once lovely, manicured grounds of which Papa had been so proud were now sadly overgrown. There were leaks in the roof which was badly in need of repair and I was running out of money. When I had to call Mr. McCullough, the local plumber, to fix the downstairs toilet, and had to offer to pay him with a piece of jewelry, I knew things were getting tight. After that, I started selling off little pieces of jewelry, a few of the smaller Tiffany lamps, fur coats, telling myself all the while that I was simply cleaning house and these were things I really didn't need. It wasn't until around 1963 that I began to understand what I was doing.

The reality was, the mansion, my Papa's pride and joy, my family home. . .was falling apart and I was running out of funds. As much as I didn't want to, I made some decisions about what I needed to do. I put the mansion up for sale.

Months passed and no buyer. Oh, there were plenty of lookers. Everyone had always wanted to see inside the "the Brown mansion," and walk around all the land we owned. I told the realtor only serious buyers could come out, but there were gawkers all the same. I hated it. I had agonized over selling the mansion, knowing that this would break Papa's heart. What else could I do, though? I started going through magazines with house plans and tried to choose one with enough square feet to meet my needs. Then came the decision of where to have my new, much smaller home built. That put me in another quandary. I was so accustomed to a secluded life. Could I live in a regular neighborhood, full of people? Neighborhoods with tiny little box shaped yards and chain link fences enclosing everything? The thought made me sick. *Oh Lord, surely there is something I can do,* I agonized.

One day I received a letter in the mail from a man, in Kansas City. On his way through Coffeyville, he had seen the "For Sale" sign in the yard and wanted to enquire about what I would be selling from inside the mansion, as he and his wife wanted to furnish their home in antiques. He wanted to offer me a price that would include everything I didn't want to move. I filed the letter away and decided if the house sold, I would get in touch with him. I certainly couldn't take all the furniture with me. It would be entirely too much for the ranch-style home I was looking to build, even though, by some standards, it still would be relatively large.

Spring turned into summer and still, no serious buyers. I was starting to consider selling the house to an institution that had shown interest in turning the mansion into a boarding school. The thought of children living in the house was quite appealing. I actually even considered it for a while, mulling it over and over in my head. I had told the lady who contacted me that I needed some time to decide exactly what I wanted to do and she understood. I didn't want to do anything in haste. Every time I would get close to making some kind of final decision on the boarding school idea, my mind would flash back to things my father had said over the years about this being "our land," "our home," and I would lose my resolve.

By the fall of 1963, I realized I would have to sell something immediately and with much regret and a heavy heart, I decided to sell the house in Machias. It sold immediately, to a wonderful family from Connecticut, an attorney, and his family. They would love the house as I had for over fifteen years. It would be in good hands. I handled the entire transaction over the phone, as I could not bear the thought of going once again to Machias, but knowing it would be my last time to see the ocean and the house I loved.

That took care of me for a while. Then, a few years later, I sold some of the land south of the mansion to a development corporation out of Wichita. They developed it into a mobile home park and gave it the name, "Mansion Estates." The first thing I did after realizing it would be rezoned for a trailer park was to plant a row of trees to try to hide this from my view. But, I knew it was there, regardless. The selling of that land and seeing those mobile homes on a daily basis was a constant reminder of how disappointed my father would be if he knew what I had done. I felt as if I had failed him somehow. But the worst part was that because of the upkeep on my aging home, I still wasn't in much better shape than before I had sold the land.

Recently, I had suffered from a terrible flu that had been going around town, and I was so sick I couldn't get out of bed. Hours had passed and Mildred hadn't come to check on me and I knew something must be terribly wrong. I managed to pull on my robe and walk on shaky legs, calling for her as I approached her room. The servant's dining room from years past had been Mildred's room for several years. *Maybe Mildred's sick, too.* I thought worriedly, as I made my way to the kitchen doorway. Past the kitchen, I could see into the doorway of her room. Mildred lay there on the floor, eyes wide and staring at the ceiling, her face a chalky white. She was dead. Even in my dazed condition, I practically ran straight to the wall phone that hung in the kitchen and dialed Lemon's number. Lemon always knew what to do.

The doctors said Mildred had suffered a fatal heart attack. I had never felt so alone in all my life.

Chapter XXIX

"Miss Violet, don't you think it's time to put the photo album back on the shelf?" Lemon asked. "You must be awfully tired."

"I am, Lemon. I'm so very tired. Looking at these old pictures sure brings it all back, doesn't it?"

"There's a lot of history in that old dusty book, that's for sure."

"It just makes me so sad, Lemon, so awfully sad. My life is practically over and what do I have left to show that I was even here? What did I contribute to the world? Nothing, that's what. I never even brought a healthy child into the world to leave behind as my legacy. My life has been nothing but a waste."

"Oh, now, don't you say that. You've been an inspiration to many women over the years, Miss Violet. You were brave enough to rid yourself of men that weren't worthy of you, and then you went on and got your college degree. Why, I think that's a lot to be proud of right there. Not many women have that kind of strength. Your Papa thought the sun rose and set in you, and your Momma never could have made it after little Donald died without all your love and support. You just quit now. You're just tired and worn out, and you've gotten yourself all depressed looking at that old dusty book full of pictures. I'm going to put it away now and fix us a good supper. After supper, we'll turn on the T.V. and watch us some shows to make us laugh, and everything will look brighter in the morning. I can just feel it."

"You're right, Lemon. I do have a headache, so maybe a nap would help. Don't let me sleep too long though. I've got to figure out what I'm going to do about everything. And I've got to do it, soon!"

Darby and his friends had planned an end-of-summer camp-out at the river. School was starting next week and this would be the last Friday night of summer vacation. With excitement and anticipation, they packed all their gear for an overnight camp-out. Sleeping bags, tent, fishing poles, hot dogs, pop and rope to make a swing, were all gathered and loaded into the back of Darby's mom's station wagon. Around town, Darby, and his mother went, gathering up all the friends that would have their end-of-summer fling at the river. Soon, they were all gathered in the car, chattering and laughing, and talking all at the same time. The spot on the river they had chosen to spend the night was east and north of the mansion.

The boys were unloaded, along with their gear, and assurances given to Darby's mom that they would be careful. She would come back the next morning to pick them up. They set up their camp and went about the task of setting up the tent, starting a fire for their evening cookout, and finding the perfect branch to hang the rope for swinging out into the water. The boys swam and fished until they were exhausted and then started their meal of hot dogs and bottles of soda pop.

The sun was setting as they sat on the bank of the river after eating; feeling completely sated by their afternoon and the food they had eaten. Each boy was looking forward to the darkness of evening and the traditional telling of ghost stories around the campfire.

They added firewood to the crackling fire pit and all moved into position on their sleeping bags that had been spread in a circle around the outer most edges of the flames. Now, came the ritual of all camp-outs; the roasting of marshmallows. After sticky fingers had been washed off at the river's edge they gathered on their sleeping bags to relax and talk about their day's events.

"It's time for the stories," Shane said, with an excited gleam in his eyes.

"Not yet," said Buz. "It's not dark enough."

"Sure it is," piped Chris. "You're just scared."

"Am not," insisted Buz.

"Okay you guys, cut it out," Darby interjected, always the peacemaker.

"Shane's right...it's time to begin. Who wants to tell the first story?"

Everyone spoke up at once, sure that his story would be the favorite one of the night.

"We'll choose who goes first with pebbles. Smallest pebble goes first, then up from there. Sound fair?" Darby had taken over years earlier as leader of their little group.

With the pebbles chosen from the river's edge and the size determining each boy's turn at storytelling, the night truly began. Shane went first.

"Well, my story begins with a tale told long ago about two old witches," Shane began. "The witches live in a big house on the far edge of town. The house is grown over with vines and weeds, and they keep dogs on the grounds to protect them from the townspeople sneaking up on them and catching them practicing their black magic and casting spells. They have long hair, all the way down their backs and ending at their knees. Their teeth are rotted out. It's been said that these two witches have cast spells on the town's most prominent citizens and caused them to go crazy. These witches have been angry with the town for years, blaming the town for all their sorrows. According to the legend, they blame the people of the town for the deaths of their loved ones.

One of the old witches had a son who died in the house when he was still very young. She believes he died because of the townspeople's hatred of her, that someone had put a spell on him. The son of this witch was sick for a long time and had to spend all his time in bed and the two witches had to care for him. All he could do to entertain himself was read and draw pictures. He soon grew tired of drawing pictures on paper and reading, and began to draw pictures all over the walls of his room. He became angry at his illness and the pictures began to take on this anger. Every part of the walls was covered in his angry drawings. He became sicker and sicker, and finally, one day he died.

When the witches came up to take his supper to him that night, he lay there dead in his bed and from the walls an eerie glow lit the room. As they stood there and looked, the walls began seeping blood. The blood flowed down the walls and onto the floor. They rushed out of the room and the blood trailed after them. It chased them out of the room and down the stairwell. The witches were screaming and crying. They couldn't even bury the boy because they couldn't get up the stairs to his room. They would slip and slide on the bloody stairs.

He's still up there in his room dead in his bed, and the witches work day and night on their spells and incantations against the townspeople for their hatred of the witches and the one witch's son. They're up there now, working their spells. They're right up there at that big house on the hill…the witches live at the Brown mansion!"

Shane grinned from ear to ear as the full impact of the story began to sink in to each individual boy around the fire.

"No way," exclaimed Chris in a whispered voice.

"It's true, man." Shane said. "My dad told me that his dad told him when he was little."

"I've heard about those witches," Buz declared. "I think it's true."

Their eyes were huge and their breath was coming in short little exhalations.

"Wanna go see?" Darby said bravely. "I know where there's a hole in the fence."

They looked from one to the other, no one brave enough to agree first.

"Come on you guys," Chris said bravely. "Let's go check it out."

They walked along the river's edge and up the small rise to the fence that surrounded the mansion. The only light came from the moon and the outline of the house loomed menacingly before them. When they got to the hole in the fence that Darby had told them about, they all hesitated, looking from one to the other.

"Are you guy's coming, or not?" Darby asked, as he struggled to separate the fence in two where the opening was, about waist high. With excitement, but almost reluctantly, the boys went through one after the other. A stillness crept over each one as they considered what they were doing. They quietly slipped through the overgrown brush and vines onto the old path to the house. So far, no dogs announced that unwanted visitors had entered the property. But, as they rounded the last turn before the house would be in full view, the dogs caught their scent and the barking began. The boys scattered in different directions.

Violet

Darby ran to the side of an old outbuilding and crouched down in the weeds. He listened as the barking of the dogs receded down toward the fence that led to the river. There was no sound of any of the other boys.

He knew he was alone.

He began to creep toward the back door of the mansion, and just as he was about to gain access to the porch, the back door flew open and there stood an old woman. Darby froze.

"Who's out there?" Violet called. Darby stood frozen to the step unable to utter a sound.

"Tell me who you are and I won't shoot," Violet said.

"It's me…uh…it's me, Darby, your paperboy," Darby said in a voice that he hoped the old woman would find non-threatening.

"Come into the light where I can see you," Violet demanded.

Darby stepped into the weak light of the overhanging porch light. There, he stood as still as possible, scared out of his wits.

"Young man, what are you doing on my property?" Violet asked.

"We're having a camp-out before school starts, down at the river. We didn't mean any harm, ma'am," Darby pleaded.

"That doesn't answer my question, young man. What are you doing up here on my land?" Violet said, not willing to let him off the hook, yet.

"We were telling stories, ghost stories, and…" Darby trailed off.

About that time, Lemon's shadow loomed behind Violet in the doorway and Darby thought he should just turn around and bolt as fast as he could for the hole in the fence. He wondered where the dogs had gone.

"Sit down right there on the porch young man and don't move a muscle. I'll be right back," Violet said, in her most threatening old-lady voice.

"Lemon, make sure he doesn't move. I've got something for this trespasser." Violet winked at Lemon as she turned toward her and headed back into the kitchen. When she came back out onto the porch she held something in her hand. She sat down beside Darby and held something out to him. He could see in the moonlight what it was. . . a bottle of grape NEHI.

"Now, let's just you and me have a little talk," Violet coaxed. "Why is it that you and your friends would want to invade the privacy of a couple of old women?"

"We thought you were witches," Darby said in a shaky voice.

"Witches?" Violet laughed. "That's good. Did you hear that, Lemon? They think we're a couple of witches."

"I heard, Miss Violet," Lemon said, from the doorway.

"What on earth would give you boys that idea?" Violet enquired.

"There's a legend about you," Darby said earnestly.

"Is that so? And what exactly is that legend?" Violet asked, genuinely interested.

"That two old witches live in this mansion," Darby explained. "And they want revenge on the townspeople for the death of one of their son's who died here."

"Oh, I see," Violet said softly. "Somehow that story has gotten a little twisted over the years, Darby. First of all, Lemon and I are not witches and we don't cast spells. We're just a couple of tired old women. I rather imagine that the boy in the story would be my little brother, Donald, who became very sick when he was about your age and died of diabetes. It's true, he was sick and he did have to spend most of the time in bed, but he didn't really die here like people like to think. He died out in California, where we had taken him, my momma and I, to a clinic, to hopefully get better. He didn't get better though. He died out there and we brought him back home on a very, very long train ride from California to Kansas." Violet's voice had taken on a faraway tone.

"I'm sorry for scaring you," Darby said sincerely.

"It's all right, Darby. I wasn't scared. I've lived out here a very long time, and Lemon and I have each other to keep from getting scared." She grinned back at Lemon who still stood sentry in the doorway. At the tone of the conversation, Lemon turned and shuffled back into the kitchen, leaving Darby and Violet to visit on the porch.

"Although, seeing you makes me realize how much I've missed my brother, all these years," Violet said longingly. "He was way too young to be taken. That was back before they knew what to do for people with diabetes. He would have lived if he had been blessed to be born in modern times. I wonder what he would have been like if he could have grown to manhood?" Violet murmured wistfully.

"You loved your brother a lot, didn't you?" Darby stated.

"Oh, my, yes. He was a beautiful boy; so full of life and spirit. You would have liked him. He was adventurous, like you. I have a feeling you two would have had quite a time together. He used to ice-skate right there on that pond," Violet said as she motioned through the trees to the tiny pond, sparkling in the moonlight. "And, he loved building little engines and figuring out how things worked. Yes, he was quite a boy. How old are you, Darby?"

"I'm eleven, ma'am," Darby answered.

"Eleven. That's all the older Donald ever got. Only eleven years old..." Violet thought for a moment and then said, "Darby, I want you to do something for me, all right?"

"Sure thing, anything," Darby replied eagerly.

"I want you to go back and tell your friends about Donald. I want you to tell them all about him and how special he was. And, I want you to live to be an old man with a whole heart full of memories and experiences. I want you to be healthy and strong, happy and content. This life is not meant for cowards, and you've shown yourself to be most brave this evening. Courage and bravery are fine attributes in a man. Will you go on now and promise me you'll have the best life you can and do it for a little boy who never got to?"

"I can do that, I sure can," Darby answered solemnly.

"Thank you, Darby," Violet said, as she reached out to shake Darby's small hand.

"For what, ma'am?"

"For giving me the chance to remember something I had lost sight of there for awhile," Violet answered. "You go on now and get back to your friends." Darby stood and shook Violet's hand and handed her the now empty bottle of grape pop.

"Thank you for the pop," Darby said shyly.

"Oh, you're so welcome," Violet said as she waved goodbye. Darby could hardly wait to get back to the campfire and tell the guy's what had happened.

Violet retired to bed feeling very old and very tired. Her talk with the young boy on the porch had brought back so many feelings she thought had been long buried by the years. Oh, how she missed her family. They had all loved each other so much. She trudged slowly to her room and sank down onto the bed. *I'm so tired,* she thought to herself as she lay back on the pillows. She closed her eyes and waited for sleep to take her. It wasn't long and she drifted off.

And, she began to dream.

There was Papa, and Momma, Donald and Willie. They were smiling. The wind was blowing through their hair and they looked so happy. They were standing by the fishpond down at the bottom of the garden. There was a feeling directed towards her of pure love and goodness. She could *feel* their love! And she could feel something else too. She could feel their pride. They were *proud of her!*

And then they were gone.

Violet woke in the darkness and smiled. Was it a dream, or had she been visited by her family? She fell back to sleep feeling a peace she had never experienced before.

She knew now what she would do about the future.

Chapter XXX

When the pale sky of early morning reached the sunrise of a new day, I rose from my bed, put on my robe and slippers and gingerly opened the door, stepping out into the hallway. I could smell the aroma of fresh bread as I moved toward the kitchen.

There's something I have to do, first. I turned around and headed back to the stairs. I reached out and grasped the railing of the stairwell and began to ascend. I stopped in front of my parents' bedroom door. *It's time,* I thought. Shaking my head in affirmation, I twisted the doorknob to the right and the door squeaked open. Once in the darkened room, I walked with purpose toward the windows. One by one, I opened the shades. The room burst into sunlight. Then, I turned around, walked out of the room, and headed down the hallway to Donald's bedroom where I repeated the process.

These rooms have been closed long enough, and it's time to let life back into them again, I whispered to myself.

I walked back to the stairs. Everything looked so bright this morning, so fresh. Even the curtains on the stairwell window looked as though they had only been hung yesterday. *I'm seeing everything with new eyes,* I thought, and smiled to myself.

Entering the kitchen, Lemon was moving toward the oven, huge mitts on each hand.

"Been up awhile, Lemon?" I knew the answer to that question as Lemon had always been an early riser.

"Lord, yes, Miss Violet; I bet I've been up and down three times since we went to bed." Lemon said, shaking her head slowly back and forth.

"Smells good in here. Is that something special in the oven?"

"I made us some cinnamon bread. Thought it might hit the spot this morning."

"That, it will," I said, as I lowered myself down into one of the two chairs that remained at the small kitchen table.

"I've got coffee all ready, too." Lemon offered, as she removed the bread from the oven and turned and looked my direction.

"You look different this morning, Miss Violet. I can't say exactly what it is, but just different somehow." Lemon looked pleased, but puzzled.

"I am different this morning, Lemon. Something unbelievable happened to me, last night."

"What do you mean, unbelievable?"

"I had a dream, Lemon; a dream about my family. It was almost as if it wasn't a dream at all, but something altogether supernatural. I've never had that happen to me before. Is that possible, Lemon?"

"I believe it is. The Lord works in mysterious ways."

"Well, I believe the Lord has finally given me my answer, Lemon."

Lemon stopped at the edge of the table, coffeepot still hovering in her hand. As she efficiently poured she said, "And what would that answer be, Miss Violet?"

"I'm so excited, Lemon, I can hardly wait to tell you." I exclaimed. "It was like a revelation, Lemon, truly it was. I know just what to do now. And the best part of all is that I don't have to worry about disappointing anyone, anymore." The last sentence was said with downcast eyes, but then quickly looking up again, I smiled broadly as I said, "Are you ready to hear about it, Lemon?"

"Lord, Miss Violet, you look about twenty years old right now with that gleam in your eye. What are you up to, and is it going to involve me casting any spells?" She laughed as she reached for the coffee. They had both gotten quite a chuckle out of Darby's visit.

"Okay, Lemon, get ready...I'm going to sell the mansion to the City of Coffeyville! They already have a museum dedicated to the Dalton raid. This would be perfect. They would have the mansion Papa built and it could be a museum, too. I would sell them everything, the house, the land, and every piece of furniture in the house. What do you think?" Everything had just burst out in one long breath.

"Well, let me see. You want to sell the house to the City, the land too, all the furniture. Where are you going to live?" Lemon asked, softly, as she raised her cup to her mouth.

"Oh, that's the best part, Lemon. That will be part of the deal. I get to stay right here until the day I die, and then the mansion becomes the property of the City."

Lemon slowly placed her cup on the table and looked earnestly across the table. "I think it's a grand idea, Miss Violet. When I think of all your Papa did for this town way back when, it seems perfectly appropriate. Best of all, he would love it as well. . . people from all over the world touring his grand mansion.

"Actually, the best part is that the mansion will always be taken care of, Lemon. That is, if the City is interested in my plan."

"Oh, they'll be interested all right, don't you worry about that. My, yes, that's a fine idea."

"I think I'll call my attorney right after breakfast and see what he thinks of the idea."

"It's perfect, just perfect." Lemon smiled.

"Lemon, would you think me an old fool if I got a little sentimental for a moment?" I asked, almost shyly.

"I've never thought of you as foolish in any way, Miss Violet." Lemon answered.

"Lemon," I said, thoughtfully, "you're the best friend I've ever had. As a matter of fact, you're more than a friend. You've supported my ideas, helped me when I was in trouble, you've just always been here for me. I want you to know you're the dearest person I've ever known. You've been in my life since I was just a young thing, and Lemon...I love you with all my heart."

Lemon was taken aback for a moment. She reached across the table and took hold of my hand. There we sat with the morning sun streaming in through the windows, two old women, hands joined, tears in their eyes.

"I love you too, Violet, always have." Lemon said.

"You know what, Lemon?" I said as I brushed the tears away with my other hand. "There'll be frost on the pumpkins, soon. You know how much we love that time of year."

"That's a fact, Miss Violet, it most certainly is," replied Lemon, patting my hand and smiling her biggest, brightest, Lemon smile.

I opened the French doors and walked out onto the veranda. I sat down in my rocker and looked out over the land as I had a thousand times before. I didn't feel discouraged, anymore. I didn't feel anxious or worried. Rocking slowly back and forth, I looked out at all the land that had belonged to my family. My mother's greenhouse that had given her such joy, the gardens where she had worked so hard, the fishpond that Donald had loved, the stables where Papa had given me my beloved pony when I was seven years old. This home and this land had meant so much to my family. Oh, the times we had shared, the love we had for one another.

"It will never be forgotten now." I thought. "All Papa and Momma worked for, it won't be forgotten." Tears welled up again as I thought of my family and how much they had meant to me.

It's true what they say about love. When it's all said and done, it's not what you've had or haven't had in your lifetime…it's the *love* that you take with you.

We were the Browns. I smiled through my tears. *We were the Browns!*

EPILOGUE

Lemon, accompanied by her son, Grant, and his little daughter, stood gazing down at the beautiful brown granite headstone where there was a bouquet of flowers on the grave. The flowers were small zinnias and some very orange marigolds, made even more garish by the "vase," a grape NEHI pop bottle. She smiled.

She imagined that there had been many flowers at the funeral. Violet loved flowers and many of her friends could afford large, beautiful displays. Lemon had been out of town visiting her grandchildren when word had come of Violet's passing. So today, she had purchased a dozen yellow roses with purple ageratum and baby's breath. She carefully placed the dark green vase, weighted with small glass marbles to keep it from tipping over, on the grave. The sunlight glinted on her diamond ring and the gold and coral bracelet left to her by Violet. It was hard to keep from crying. There was so much left unsaid; so much that should have come to pass and yet had failed. That was the worst part about saying good-bye to Violet. She deserved to have had a wonderful life, yet in many ways it seemed that she had been cheated at every turn.

Her brothers had died so young. Her parents were gone. Her only child had lived just five days. Her husbands, well. . . "Poor Violet," Lemon murmured softly. She reached into her pocket and fingered the yellowed piece of paper that rested there. She had found this among Violet's many postcards and trinkets. It had obviously been saved over many years.

> Walk with the Sun,
> Dance at high Noon;
> And dream when night falls black;
> But when the Stars
> Vie with the Moon,
> Then call the lost dream back.

Lemon thought about Violet, Mr. and Mrs. Brown, Donald, even little Willie and the mansion. She thought of the mansion, and remembered the laughter that had filled its rooms. She purposely did not remember the sorrows or the painful moments, just the good memories. And, my, there had been so many good memories.

And, now, because of Violet's gift, strangers would come through the mansion every day. Most, she knew, would be impressed by the beauty of the mansion, and what they would think must have been such a glamorous life for its inhabitants in this little Kansas town.

Lemon gazed over the row of headstones, and then back to Violet's…the last of the Browns. It is true, she thought, Violet had walked with the sun, she had danced at high noon; and she had dreamed when the night fell black. But, when life had seemed uncompromising in its unhappiness, in her own way, Violet had called the lost dream back and had given new life to the mansion.

Slowly, Lemon moved away from Violet's grave, she looked back and saw Grant's little daughter, Vi, take a red rose from the vase of flowers she had brought for Violet and place it on Donald's grave. Violet would like that.

Printed in the United States
93272LV00002B/301-315/A